# Taking the Ice 2

## Skate Like No One's Watching

Allye M. Ritt

ISBN 978-1-63885-070-0 (Paperback)
ISBN 978-1-63885-071-7 (Digital)


First Edition



Covenant Books, Inc.
11661 Hwy 707
Murrells Inlet, SC 29576
www.covenantbooks.com

# CHAPTER 1

## *Wrapped in a Dream*

I try to pull my blanket over my face and give up after realizing how tightly it's tangled around my legs. As a backup plan, I roll face-first into my pillow. The sun is so bright this morning. It's glaring through my windows, my plastic blinds and sheer ballet slipper pink curtains incapable of muffling the majority of light.

I have zero desire to get out of bed. Normally I rise early with the opportunity to go to the rink and work towards my dream. But not today. Not ever again, it sometimes seems…

Last night I had another skating dream. Perhaps by lying here, I'll be able to extend the reality of the dream. Skating dreams are the best, but they can also be fairly aggressive, thus the tangled blankets. I jump and spin in my dreams, and apparently, I jump and spin in my bed as well. My blankets are always a mess when I wake from a skating dream.

How I yearn to be back at the rink! What I would give to wake up at 4:30 a.m. for a skating lesson! I can't stop thinking about the feel of the ice beneath my feet.

It's been over a week since I passed my first official figure skating test. I worked for several months preparing for that test, and I'm still in shock that I actually passed it! I am now officially tested at the national level. But does that even matter now? It makes no difference if I can't ever go to the rink again!

I'm so anxious to start preparing for my next test already and for the ice show. But I haven't been able to work with Coach Marie since the day of the test session. The only skating I'm doing is in my dreams.

Mom and Dad asked Coach Marie to give me some time off, but they didn't talk to me about it first. This has made me furious—I don't want to take a break! I want to keep going. I want to be as good as skaters like Yana, Tamerah, and Stacy. I can't understand why my parents would put a pause on my progress like this. Logic suddenly runs through my mind despite all my feelings and frustrations; maybe I should just go ask Mom right now…

This is a reason to get out of bed. This answer is more important to me than anything right now.

I untangle my blankets from my legs. It's almost like I was actually doing the double jumps of my dreams in my bed! Wow! What a tangled mess!

I quickly change out of my pyjamas and jog down the steps. I find my mom working on her laptop at the kitchen table.

"Good morning, Khalli honey! You slept late, I bet that felt refreshing on a Saturday morning," Mom says with a gentle smile.

I try to smile back but decide not to answer. How could I possibly feel refreshed when my skating dream is crumbling around me?

I pause as I consider exactly what I'm going to say. I want to phrase my words as maturely as possible. I don't want to make my mom angry, but I also want to know why I haven't been able to have a lesson or practice. My mom listens, takes a minute to formulate what she's going to say, and begins.

"Khalli, we are so proud of you! And we want you to know that we did everything we could to help you get to the point where you are now. However, lessons cost money. A lot of money. An hour-long lesson with Marie costs over seventy dollars, and even though we fully believe she is worth that rate, and you have made so much progress with her, we cannot afford to continue with extra lessons. We didn't want to worry you until we had a solution, which is why we haven't said much other than that you are taking a short break. But as of last night, we've talked with Marie and have some options for you."

I already don't like the way this sounds. This is my dream! I don't want options—I want lessons and ice time! What about the ice show? What about the competition? I want to take my next test. How will that ever happen now?

I decide not to interrupt Mom. The quicker she gets to the point, the sooner I will know my fate.

"So these are your options. Option 1, I can schedule ninety minutes of lessons with Marie for you each week. Option 2, Marie has an upper-level student who will be home for spring break and summer. She is just starting to coach, so her rate is less than half that of Marie's. I can schedule three hours a week with her as your coach when she's here. Or the final option, I can schedule an hour with Marie and one hour with Jessica—that's Marie's student. What do you think?"

I can't process this right now. I need more time to think!

"When do I need to decide? And when will I have my next lesson?" I ask.

At least this isn't going to be the end of my skating. But I really love working with Coach Marie—I don't want a new coach.

"I have a lesson scheduled with Marie on Monday for thirty minutes before school. I'm sorry your dad and I needed you to take a break, but your dad had his hours cut short for the last two weeks, and then money got tight because we invested so much extra into your lessons last month. We weren't expecting his hours to be cut, and we had to dip into our savings. We want you to know that you are worth it, but we also need to make sure you always have a roof over your head and have food to eat. We're fine, but we needed some time to work out our new budget before we spent more than we could afford to. You understand, right?"

"I do. But I also know that this is my dream… Let me think about my options a little, okay, Mom?"

"Of course, Khalli. But thank you for asking and for letting me explain. It's good we talked today because now, if you'd like, you can talk to Coach Marie about Jessica in your lesson on Monday," Mom says with a tired smile.

I walk to my room to work out in front of my mirror. I find I think the most clearly when I am practicing what I love. I'm happy that I will still get to skate, but sad that I won't get two or more hours of lessons with Coach Marie each week. The extra lessons were really helping me improve quickly. My feelings are all over the place. I want to be mad at my dad's boss for cutting his hours, but I also am happy that he gave my dad extra hours before he cut them so that my parents could afford to get me extra lessons. But now that I've seen what extra lessons can do for my skating, I want more!

I realize I've been holding my opening position for my program in front of the mirror through that entire thought process. This position has gotten so much easier! Coach Marie and I finished my entire program the week before the test session. My program is set to the music from *Moana*, just like I wanted. I have five jumps—two are combinations, two spins, two spirals, a footwork sequence, and a whole bunch of connecting steps all mixed together. I really, really love the program Coach Marie created for me! I want to keep perfecting it with her, not with Jessica. I don't even know who Jessica is!

*****

"Khalli! It seems like it's been forever since I've seen you, although I guess it was only last week when you rocked your test like a star!" Coach Marie throws me a high five.

"I've missed my lessons. My mom and dad were struggling with—"

"I know. Your mom called and explained the situation to me. Your parents really want to help you reach your dreams, which is why I suggested Jessica to them. She's a beautiful skater with a lot of skating credentials to her credit—but because she's only been coaching for a year, her rate is much less. I think you'll really like her. She's very friendly and upbeat."

"Does this mean you don't want to work with me anymore?" I ask, full of worry and disappointment.

"I absolutely love working with you, Khalli. I wouldn't share you if I thought that was best for you. But with as much time as you put into practicing, you really need more than just one or two short lessons a week. I think grabbing a couple lessons with Jessica each week would be a great way to keep improving at your accelerated rate. I'd love to keep working with you. I suggested to your mom you work with us both."

"How come I don't know who she is? I've never seen her here before."

"Jessica skated here all the time for over a decade. Just before you started skating with me, she left for college. She's been studying, skating, and coaching in Minnesota all school year, but in a few weeks she is returning for spring break, some occasional weekends, and then again for the entire summer. You could work with both of us when she's home. In fall, when she's back at school, we can create a new plan as needed."

"So this isn't a forever deal?"

"This is just for the spring and summer. I take it you and your mom didn't get to talk about the timeline..."

I shake my head.

"Your mom was really worried that she wasn't going to be able to get you the lessons you needed over the summer with how much she believes you'll want to skate. Jessica will make it possible for this to happen at a much lower cost. I'll still work with you at least once a week as well. What do you think?"

I think Coach Marie already made the decision for me. And I think she made this decision with my best interests in mind, even though I would rather work only with her. She's always given me exactly what I've needed to be successful; I think I should trust her and give her plan a try.

"Okay," I say softly. "I'll try some lessons with Jessica. If I don't like her, can I change my mind?"

"Of course you can change your mind, although I don't think you will," she says with a confident face. "Jessica and I will team coach you. We'll work together to make sure you're getting exactly what you need."

I guess it's settled then. My first coaching team—Coach Marie and Jessica...whoever she is.

# CHAPTER 2

## *Mashed Potatoes and Math*

I am way more focused in school today. The beginning of last week, I was on cloud nine after passing my first skating test, but then by the end of the week, I was in a permanent state of bummed. What an emotional roller coaster!

For the last month I had been staying in for one recess each day to work on homework so that I would have more time to skate when I wasn't in school. Last week Mrs. Hill made me go out for both recesses; she said I needed to move around and gain some positive energy. I didn't even try to protest; there was no reason for me to stay inside if I didn't have skating practice. Today I asked to stay inside again. Mrs. Hill smiled and willingly agreed.

"I'm happy to see you cheerful again, Khalli. Of course you can stay inside. Does this mean everything is better at the rink again?"

I tell her yes but don't go into details—I have work to do!

I bury my head in my math assignment. Today we are working with fractions again. We worked with fractions last week, but I was so distracted by my seemingly broken dream that I didn't focus enough to understand. Hopefully, I can catch up and relearn what I missed.

I spend an entire twenty minutes on one assignment and only get through three math problems. I had to stop and reread the directions several times to figure out how to add the fractions. Why is this so hard?

I thought about asking Mrs. Hill for help but didn't want her to know how little I actually paid attention last week—although I imagine she actually knows.

While I'm trying to focus and reread the directions for the forty millionth time, the halls fill with noise as all of my classmates rush in. Recess is over. Dacia and Becky run up to my desk.

"We missed you outside today! It was so great having you outside last week for both recesses—even if you did hate your life," Becky jokes.

"What are you working on?" Dacia leans over my shoulder and peeks at my work.

"Fractions. I don't understand them at all."

"Clearly," Dacia laughs. "These are all wrong. I can help you if you'd like. I struggled with them too, until my dad explained them to me. He's an accountant, which makes him my personal math tutor."

"Really? I would love your help, Dacia!"

"Bring your math book to lunch. It's a date! A math lunch date!"

"Seriously!" Becky whips around in her seat right in front of me, where she's been listening to our entire conversation. “That’s the grossest date ever!” She twists her face into a disgusted look, but her seriousness is lost as a smile spreads across her face.

“Hi, Khalli!” she attempts to mimic Dacia’s voice while brushing her red curls off her face. “Did you bring your math book? Wow! You and your math book look lovely today. It’s been so long since the three of us have hung out together. Math book, that’s such a nice book cover you’re wearing, it really makes your pages look so fresh! Is it a designer cover? Kate Spade, maybe? What are you both ordering at this fine school cafeteria? Oh no, math book! I forgot, you don’t have any teeth—perhaps some mashed potatoes for you?”

Dacia is falling over my desk from laughing so hard at Becky, and I am practically falling out of it in hysteria. We are in such a giggle fest that we don’t even notice Mrs. Hill has approached and is standing behind us. Becky’s face suddenly goes blank, and she snaps her body straight and turns forward. Dacia and I realize immediately what this means. Dacia runs to her seat, and I sit up straight and proper. Busted!

“Ladies, I imagine you didn’t hear me when I asked you to take your silent reading books out. You will take them out immediately, or you will be late for lunch,” Mrs. Hill says sternly.

“I’m sorry,” I whisper to her as I pull out my book. I hate upsetting Mrs. Hill, she really is a great teacher and a kind person.

Mrs. Hills acknowledges that she heard me with a stiff nod of her head. She walks back to her desk, and I sink my head into my book.

*****

At lunch Dacia and I go over my math homework while Becky hangs out with two other girls from our class, Tanja and Keeloni.

Dacia is amazing at explaining things and really helps me to make sense out of fractions. She shows me how to use multiplication to make the bottom number of the fraction the same so that I can simply add the top numbers together. Why did the directions in my math book confuse me so much? This really isn't too difficult.

Dacia gives me some sample problems to work through. "I don't want to help you with the actual problems on the assignment because I don't want Mrs. Hill to think we were cheating," she explains.

I agree to her logic and work through the sample problems she gives me. I get them all correct, which is fantastic, but now I still need to do my actual math assignment. This is like double the homework! Ugh! I shouldn't complain though; at least I understand how to add fractions now!

# CHAPTER 3

## *Positive Habits*

I jump out of my bed and rush to get dressed. I want to make my mom breakfast before she takes me to the rink. Until I learned how much effort my parents put in to keep me skating, I guess I'd never really thought about how much they did for me. I thought my success was because of my effort. And obviously I put in the work, but so did my parents to pay for everything and to wake up early to take me to the rink.

"Something smells fantastic!" Mom swoons as she comes down the stairs towards the kitchen.

"I made scrambled eggs for you. I also made some for Dad, but they will be cold before he wakes up. Be careful and watch for eggshells though, I struggled cracking one of the eggs."

"Khalli, honey, this is wonderful!"

"I just want to say thank you, Mom. I know my skating is expensive, and I know you and Dad are working extra hard to make it possible. I love you, guys!"

Mom wipes a small tear from her eye—she's kind of a softie, as my dad always jokes. Lots of tears for lots of reasons.

Mom wraps me in her arms and squeezes. I give her a minute before I gently shake her off.

"Your eggs are getting cold! And we have to get to the rink so I can practice."

Mom lets go and sits down to eat her eggs. I pour her a glass of orange juice and then rush off to finish getting ready.

*****

At the rink, Yana greets me while we stretch. I didn't get to talk to her yesterday morning and am excited to have a chance today.

"Two days in a row, Khalli! I see you are back at it again."

"A week without skating was hard for me. I missed it!"

"I have the same struggle," Yana tells me.

"How did your test go? Did you pass? I'm sorry I didn't stay to watch you."

"I did pass…but barely. I had a rough skate. Normally I can control my nerves, but last week I really struggled. I think it's because I spent the entire day at the rink. Maybe next time I should leave in between tests."

"I'm glad you passed, Yana! And I'm glad you stayed to cheer me on—that helped me, even if it meant a long day at the rink for you."

"I wouldn't have missed it! Coach Marie says you're a star!" Yana smiles at me.

How did I make such a cool and nice friend? Yana makes me feel as good about skating as Coach Marie!

Coach Marie approaches as we stretch. "Khalli, while you're stretching, let's stretch out your spirals together."

I used to hate this, but now I smile at the opportunity.

"Absolutely! Can you help me push my leg up a little higher? I've been stretching like crazy at home, but my mom isn't always available to help push my leg up."

"Of course I will! You are one of the few skaters who appreciates this torture!" Coach Marie says with a big smile.

My coach stands behind me and pushes my leg up over my head. She holds my leg at its max to help me stretch, and then after she lets go, she starts counting down from ten. I can feel my leg shaking as I fight to hold my position.

"Is it any higher?" I ask. It definitely feels higher.

"It sure is! Great job stretching at home!" Coach Marie applauds me. "Today I want to start learning the patterns for your next test as well as run through your program for the competition and ice show. We only have thirty minutes, but you catch on really quickly, so let's see how far we can get. We'll pick apart your technique a lot more next time. My goal for today is to give you something to practice on your own and to think about. Sound good?"

"Sounds great!"

We start out with a pattern that involves a lot of crossovers. Crossovers are exactly as they sound. You cross one foot over the top of the other. This is all done with a lot of strong pushes so that you gain speed as you glide across the ice. In this pattern I will have to do both forward crossovers and backward crossovers. Coach Marie and I spent a ton of time cleaning up my technique over the last month—she warned me that these crossovers were going to show up on a test soon. I'm glad I worked so hard on them. Because of my hard work, this pattern isn't too hard.

"Not bad for your first try! When you practice these by yourself, I want you to remember a few things. We've talked about all of this before. First, I want your arms to be strong. If you hug the circle you are making on the ice with your arms, they will be in the correct place. Remember to keep your palms down too."

Oh shoot! I totally forgot about the arms. I make a mental note to fix them next time.

"Second, watch out for toe pushes on the forward crossovers. Do you remember how we worked to turn your foot sideways on the push, keeping your toe from digging into the ice?"

I nod my head. How could I forget? We spent a ton of time fixing this on my last test. But I did forget…

"Your knee bend is really good. Keep working to stay down on your knees through the entire pattern. I want you to aim to bend from the ankles, press your shins forward against your boots, this will help you bend your knees without your butt sticking out. I know you had a lot to think about for your first time doing this, a lot of these little mistakes will fade as proper technique becomes a habit. Your job is to remember to fix these errors when you practice on your own. When I see you next, I expect to see some progress. Do you have any questions about the pattern?"

"Nope—I will try to fix these things before our next lesson," I tell my coach confidently.

"I know you will," she smiles. "Now let's go onto your next pattern. It's another spiral pattern, much more difficult than the one on your last test. Are you ready for the challenge?"

"Absolutely!"

"Why would I even ask?" Coach Marie says with a laugh. "All right! Here we go!"

We get through three full patterns for my next test in our lesson, and then I skate through my program. Coach Marie gives me some small corrections after I strike my end pose, and I promise to make corrections on my own. I wish I had more time to work with my coach—I feel like I learned so much today! My next lesson isn't until Friday, but I plan to come practice everything she taught me today, on my own.

# CHAPTER 4

## *My Kind of Project*

At school Mrs. Hill assigns us a big project.

"You are each going to report on a historical figure. I want you to choose a person who not only interests you, but also be sure that the actions of this person impacted you and the world in some way. This person could be a past president, an explorer, a king or queen, an actor, a musician, a major league baseball player, a soldier, an activist for human rights, a—"

"Mrs. Hill! What's an activist?" Gio loudly interrupts. He tends to do this…a lot.

"Gio, what have I said about interrupting?" Mrs. Hill sternly turns to Gio.

"That it's rude and shows my inability to control myself. That I should raise my hand instead and that you will always make sure to answer my questions," Gio mechanically states. He's been asked this multiple times before.

"Good. I am more than happy to answer your question, but you will be staying in my room three minutes into recess for your outburst."

"Sorry, Mrs. Hill," Gio mutters.

"Apology accepted, thank you, Gio. Now class, Gio had a very good question! Who can tell me what or who an activist is?" Mrs. Hill always has the ability to call someone out for their mistakes but at the same time praise them for something else. She'd make a great figure skating coach!

Keeloni raises her hand, and Mrs. Hill calls on her.

"An activist is a person who stands up for what they believe. Someone who tries to change the world and fix problems or unfairness, like Rosa Parks."

"Very good, Keeloni! Can you tell us who Rosa Parks is?"

"Rosa Parks was an African American woman riding on a bus. Back in that time, buses were divided between white people, who got the better seats, and black people, who had to sit in the back. When all the seats for white people filled up, the bus driver made the black people stand to make more seats for the white people. Rosa Parks refused to move from the bus seat she paid for, because of this she is considered a civil rights activist. She stood up for the rights of black people in America."

"Very, very good, Keeloni!"

"Thank you, Mrs. Hill. My mom says learning the history of African Americans is important. She says we can learn so much from others, especially the importance of standing up for ourselves and others. She says all history is important, but I should make sure to learn mine."

"Keeloni, you just told your classmates the importance of this assignment and the reason we learn history in school.

That was very well said. You and your mother are smart women, the kind of women who will make a difference in this world."

Keeloni beams with pride. "Thank you, Mrs. Hill."

Mrs. Hill goes on to tell us we will not only research our person of interest, but we will also dress up like that person for a presentation. We are supposed to talk in the first-person point of view. That means talking about the person while pretending that we are the person, saying "I am…" or "I did…"

Who should I be?

Mrs. Hill passes out laptop computers and a sheet of paper with the project requirements. On the back side there is a list of all of the different types of people we can choose from. I scan over the list, and my eyes come to an immediate halt over the words *professional athlete.* Could I research a figure skater? I could wear my beautiful skating dress for my presentation! This might just be the coolest project ever!

*****

I stay in for the first recess again to get a start on my project. I need to figure out which figure skater I want to report on. Mrs. Hill is talking quietly to Gio by her desk while I log into my Chromebook. I type "Famous Figure Skaters" into the search bar as Gio walks past me to head outside. He gives me a confused look as he passes me. I imagine he can't figure out why I stay inside by choice.

Google gives me links upon links about famous figure skaters. Hmmmm, I'm going to need to narrow this down. I click on a web page about influential skaters and scroll through the lists. Some of these skaters are my favorites, some I've never heard of before. I'm shocked at how many Olympic gold medalists I've never known about!

I recognize some of the skaters' names listed for the 1998 Olympics in Nagano, Japan. It's the earliest year I recognize skaters. Year 1998 was way before I was born. I'm impressed I know so many names: Tara Lipinski, the youngest Olympic gold medalist ever in ladies' figure skating; she announces on TV a lot; Michelle Kwan, I've read about her in my figure skating magazine. But most of the other names I've never heard of—I have a lot of research to do!

I spend the entire recess reading about famous skaters of the past: men and women who made history and changed the sport I love. And then I saw her, backflipping across my computer screen: Surya Bonaly—an Olympian with three silver medals from Worlds, five European Championship golds and one silver, nine gold medals from the French Nationals and one silver. Wow! This is who I want to research! This is the influential person I want to teach my class about!

I go to YouTube and watch videos of Surya Bonaly—she is amazing! The amount of athleticism she displayed is insane—this woman is a legend!

Mrs. Hill peeks over my shoulder. "Khalli, are you working on school, or are you working on skating?"

"Both! I want to research Surya Bonaly for my project. Can I?"

"Absolutely! I don't know too much about figure skating, but I know a little about Surya Bonaly. She was incredible! I will give you some suggestions, Khalli, and you should take them because your grade will depend on it."

I'm listening now. I know that I need to keep my grades up to keep skating.

"Make sure that when you do your project, you don't just talk about Surya's skating skills. Tell us about her efforts that brought her to the top of the sport. Teach us about her recipe for success—Surya Bonaly was an amazing skater, but she didn't get to the podium overnight. In addition, there was something unique about her that set her apart—I want you to tell the class about this, because this reason impacted the next generation of skaters."

"I will be sure to figure it out. Thank you, Mrs. Hill."

"You're welcome!"

I pack up the computer and return it to its charging cart in the back of the room as my classmates return from recess. It's time for our math lesson, and I cannot wait to prove that I understand fractions!

# CHAPTER 5

## *Friends For(n)ever*

I don't have as many skating lessons as usual right now, but I still go to the rink regularly to practice. It's frustrating because when I have a question, I need to remember it until my next lesson. Coach Marie suggested I get a notebook to write my questions down so I don't forget. She also suggested I take notes on our lessons so I can remember to work on every little thing when I practice on my own.

Mom and I went to the store last night, and I picked a notebook out. On the cover is a brightly colored blue, green, and purple bird. I picked it because I feel like I'm flying, just like a bird, when I do big jumps. The background is a lavender and rose-colored swirl, which reminds me of spinning. It really is the perfect notebook for a figure skater!

I write down my first question for Coach Marie: "Where do I put my arms when I do a camel spin?"

Coach Marie and I just started working on camel spins. I know she told me, but there is so much to remember that I already completely forgot about the arms. A camel spin is basically a spiral, or arabesque, as dancers call it. Except now, rather than just holding my leg up behind me, I have to do it spinning! I know I'm not supposed to dive headfirst into the spin, yet I need to make sure my upper-body dips forward. I know my skating knee needs to be bent on the entry but then straight in the spin. It's all so technical, but I can't remember for the life of me what I'm supposed to do with my arms! This is apparently why I need a notebook!

I add another question underneath that one. It has very little to do with my lesson but a ton to do with skating!

"What do you know about Surya Bonaly?"

*****

Becky and I always walk home together after school. Today she meets me at my locker with Keeloni.

"Keeloni is going to walk home with us. She's coming to my house to hang out for the afternoon," Becky tells me.

"Oh? I didn't know you two were friends like that."

"We've been spending a lot of time together during first recess when you're inside—Dacia, Tanja, Keeloni, and me. It turns out we have a lot in common. I don't know why we didn't hang out sooner. Anyway, we needed another person to play our games since you were always inside, so we asked Keeloni and Tanja to join us."

"Oh."

The walk home feels awkward to me. My best friend is joking with Keeloni. They are trying to include me, but it seems like they have so many inside jokes that I don't understand. What is happening? Am I losing my best friend? Is it worth it, giving up time with my friends to finish my homework so I can skate?

"Do you guys want to come over to my house? I can skip off-ice training today. It's not very often that a new friend comes over. It'll be fun!" I feel like I'm forcing my enthusiasm, but I really want to be included.

"I wish I could. But I promised my mom I would stay at Becky's," Keeloni tells me.

"Okay, I'll just join you there," I invite myself.

Becky and Keeloni look at each other without saying a word. I immediately feel like I'm not wanted there.

"I'm sorry, Khalli. It's not personal, but Keeloni and I talked to Mrs. Hill, and she gave us permission to do this project as a team. We want to surprise everybody with a project that will make a difference, and we want you to be surprised too."

"But I'm your best friend. You won't even tell me?"

"I'm sorry, Khalli. You'll know soon enough—I promise!"

Becky can tell I'm upset, and I can see she doesn't want to make me feel bad. But maybe she should have thought about that before she decided to create a secret project with Keeloni!

I walk the rest of the way home, not sure if I'm going to cry or kick a hole through the pavement out of anger. How could my best friend just go and make a new friend? It's always been just Becky and me. And when it wasn't just the two of us, then it was the two of us with Dacia. Keeloni isn't part of our group; she's part of Tanja's group. I don't want another friend; I want everything to be just as it was before.

Mom looks up as I slam the front door behind me.

"Hey! We don't slam doors around here!"

I ignore her and go straight to my room. Mom, of course, isn't okay with being ignored.

"Khalli!" she yells up the steps.

Again I ignore her. I should know by now that ignoring my mom never works. Why do I even try?

Within seconds she's at my bedroom door.

"Can I come in?"

I tell her, "Not right now."

"Okay, I was trying to be respectful towards you, but 'not right now' is not an appropriate answer." Mom walks into my room anyway.

"We don't slam doors in this house. And we also don't take our anger out on each other. I love you, honey, and if something is wrong, I'd like to talk about it and see if I can help."

"You can't," I mutter, face down in my pillow.

"Try me," Mom says softly.

"Becky has a new best friend," I blurt out.

Mom waits patiently.

"She invited Keeloni over to her house. She walked home with us too. That's my time with Becky, not Keeloni's time!"

"I'm sorry, Khalli. Is this the Keeloni I've met from your class?"

I nod.

"She seems like a very nice girl. And smart too. I've talked to her parents at school events, I quite like them."

"Well, then you can go be her friend too! Why doesn't everyone who I care about just go love Keeloni instead!" I fold my arms across my chest and fight back tears.

"Did Keeloni do something to hurt you?" my mom asks concerned.

"She took my best friend, that's all." The tears are breaking free now.

"How'd she do that?"

"By being nice to Becky and Dacia while I was doing my homework at recess. I only do my homework then so I have more time to skate. I didn't mean for my friends to make new friends while I was inside working. It's not right!"

"I see," Mom says carefully. She pauses as she thinks through the situation. "Khalli, how does Becky feel about your new skating friends?"

"I don't know—I haven't asked her."

"How does she feel about you going skating in the morning instead of walking to school with her?" Mom continues with another question.

Again, I don't have an answer.

"How does she feel about you staying inside during the time you two usually hang out together? Do you think it bothers her that you're not always available to hang out when she wants to?"

I see the point that mom is trying to make.

"Mom, do you think I'm a bad friend?"

"No, honey. I think when you are with your friends, you are a very good friend. I also think you are a very determined and good skater. But I think you're learning that it's hard to be everything. It's hard to make time for your friends when you are determined to be a great athlete. You have to make sacrifices, you have to give up your free time. But just realize that your friends are making sacrifices for this too. They are giving up time with you, so you can go after your dream. Have you thought about how hard this might be for them? Have you thanked them for their support?"

I shake my head. Mom has a point. I've skipped out on a lot of events with my friends, and sometimes at the last minute, because of skating. I wonder if they think skating is more important to me than they are. They've been so supportive of me. Maybe I should be more supportive about them wanting to have other friends when I'm not available.

"I guess I am jealous. I want time alone with Becky," I tell my mom.

"I'm sure you will get that time. Becky's your best friend. But she's allowed to have other friends, just like you're allowed to have your friends at the rink. Give Keeloni a chance. Maybe you'll like her just as much as Becky does, and then you can all be friends." Mom smiles at me.

"I know you're right, but I don't want you to be. And I still don't like it, but I guess I need to get used to the idea… and I need to apologize."

My mom gives me a big hug.

"Let's go make a snack. I would enjoy some rare after-school time with my daughter," Mom says with a gentle smile as she takes my hand to pull me out of bed.

# CHAPTER 6

## *The Best, Best Friend*

Mrs. Hill gives us an entire hour of work time for our project in the morning and then another hour of work time after lunch.

"You will need to put in some time outside of school to do this project well, but I want to make sure you have enough time to ask me questions and to use the computers. You only have today, tomorrow, and then the weekend to finish. Don't forget to dress up like whoever you're researching on Monday!"

Becky and Keeloni take their laptops into the hallway to work alone together. I imagine they don't want the rest of the class knowing what they are working on. At least I kind of know what's going on, and they trusted me enough to say it's a surprise for the entire class.

I have the beginning of my presentation all figured out. When I told Yana what I was working on, she taught me how to say, "*Je m'appelle Surya Bonaly.*" This means, "My name is Surya Bonaly," in French. She takes French in middle school and is already in her second year of studying. I thought that would be the perfect start to my presentation! Yana said she really looks up to Surya because she helped pave the way for other skaters like her.

Now it's the fun part of my project—researching this incredible woman!

Surya was athletic and strong, her movements sharp and powerful. Many of the other skaters at the time were more delicate and flowy. As I watch videos of Surya, I can't help but love the athleticism she brings to the sport. I'm in awe! I'm sure Surya stood out because of this strength, but was it the only reason? What did Mrs. Hill mean when she said that something set Surya apart? I keep searching; my grade depends on it.

I pull up team photos, watch her competitors, sift through link after link of her competitions, browse documentaries, and then I finally realize what made her unique—the rest of the skaters had lighter skin. When Surya was skating, there weren't many other black figure skaters. She was an outstanding black athlete who didn't fit the image of figure skaters of the time, but she didn't let that stop her! Surya said it was difficult to be black, but it also gave her an opportunity to be unique and stand out—what a beautiful mindset to apply to diversity! And by standing out, Surya inspired people of color to give skating a try! Now I also know what Yana meant when she said Surya helped pave the way for skaters like her!

I begin writing my speech now that I have so many notes and so much information. I cannot wait to teach my classmates about this impressive woman!

*****

At the end of the day, I walk home with Becky. I've already apologized to her and the others, and we talked about why I was upset. It turns out it really did bother her that I was skating all the time and didn't have as much time with her. Mom was right! We made a promise to tell each other next time something bothers us.

"Dacia, Tanja, Keeloni, and I were talking about trying to go to the movies this weekend. There's a new Disney movie out. We want you to come! I know you don't know Keeloni and Tanja very well, but I think you'll really like them if you spend more time together. Will you come?" Becky asks me.

"I want to! When?"

"We didn't pick the showtime yet. But my mom said she's free all day Saturday and can take us. Everyone else is still checking with their parents. We thought we'd pick the showtime based on your skating schedule. What time works for you?"

"You would do that for me? You are the best!"

"It was actually Keeloni's idea. She feels bad that you thought she was trying to take me away from you. We didn't mean to upset you, and we think it's really kind that you apologized to all of us."

"I can go in the afternoon or evening. I have my first lesson with my new coach on Saturday. I'm really nervous. But I should be home by noon."

Becky asks me why I'm getting a new coach, and I explain the entire situation to her.

"Why didn't you tell me sooner?" she asks me.

"I was really upset about it and didn't walk to talk about it yet. And I didn't know if you'd even care."

"Of course I care! You're my best friend, and if you're upset, I'm upset. Even though I don't skate with you, I want to hear all about your skating life. I know it's important to you."

I really love my best friend!

I give Becky a big hug and grab her hand. I pull her along with me as I begin to hop down the sidewalk. We end up skipping together the rest of the way home, singing pop songs from the radio.

It makes me so happy to know she supports me and that she's still my best friend, even if I excluded her from all my skating stuff and made mistakes that didn't make me the greatest friend. Becky is one of the best people I know, and I plan to be her best friend forever!

# CHAPTER 7

## *Meeting Jessica*

It's Saturday morning, and I'm off to the rink for my first lesson with Jessica. Coach Marie promised to join us for the beginning of our lesson to make sure I feel comfortable. I'm still really nervous—I have no idea who Jessica is.

When I get to the rink, everyone is really excited—there's an immense buzz of energy filling the lobby. Yana, Stacy, Tamerah, and some of the other older skaters are huddled around someone. Yana runs over to me once she notices I'm there.

"Khalli, come meet Jessica!" Yana pulls me by the hand. "She used to skate here and is one of the most beautiful skaters ever. She's home on spring break from her college. She's still training, wait until you see her skate! And she's going to be coaching here as well."

"I'm going to be working with her," I tell Yana. "Today is my first lesson."

"That's going to be so great! Jessica is wonderful!"

"Jessica! Jessica!" Yana calls over to the huddle. "Wait until you meet Khalli! She's new here since you left for college."

Jessica breaks away from the huddle and approaches us. She looks friendly enough with her wavy, shoulder-length brown hair and blue eyes. She's tiny for an adult, not too much taller than I am. She gives me a huge smile and reaches to shake my hand. Most adults don't shake my hand—I'm just a kid. I like that she thinks I'm important enough for this greeting!

"Hi, Khalli! I'm Jessica. Marie has told me so much about you. I'm so excited to finally meet you and am really looking forward to helping you improve your skating."

Jessica smiles the entire time she's talking to me. I can almost see her energy! I guess Coach Marie wasn't kidding when she said Jessica was upbeat!

"Hi." I shake her hand shyly. I'm not really sure what else to say.

Coach Marie walks through the doors, her skate bag in hand.

"Jessica!" She drops her bag and gives Jessica a huge hug. And then turning to both of us, she says, "I see you two have already found each other."

*Perfect timing*, I think to myself. I was at a loss for words. I didn't want Jessica to think I didn't like her, but I really didn't know what to say.

"I can't wait to see what the two of you accomplish together. You are both some of the most hardworking skaters I've ever coached!" Coach Marie smiles.

*****

On the ice, Coach Marie joins Jessica and me.

"Jessica and I have already talked about where your strengths and weaknesses lie and where you should put your efforts. We believe your primary focus is to prepare for the competition and ice show right now, while also strengthening your single jumps and your spins and working towards your next skills test. Do you agree with this, Khalli?"

"Yes. I want to do well in the show and the competition. Over the summer I'm hoping to start working on my Axel—do you think that might happen?"

"I think it's very possible." Coach Marie smiles. "With as much as you skate and as hard as you work, I think you will make extreme progress, and I can't wait to see what you and Coach Jessica accomplish!"

I beam with pride and notice Jessica smiling as well. Actually, I don't think I've seen her without a smile yet.

Coach Marie skates away to teach her lessons and leaves me with Jessica.

"I'd like to start with your program and see you skate to your music. Since Marie did your choreography, I don't know what it looks like yet. She told me you're skating to music from *Moana* and gave me a list of elements—the jumps and spins that you do. Let's get you warmed up, and then we'll tackle your program. Does that sound like a plan?"

Wow! Coach Jessica is just like Coach Marie—she doesn't waste any time!

"That works. Coach Marie usually has me take a couple laps and then warm up with my test patterns. Should I do that?"

"That's perfect. After your laps, let's warm up your crossover pattern."

I skate off to warm up and do my absolute best technique. I want my new coach to think I'm a good skater.

"I'd like to see more knee bend and ankle bend in your crossovers, and don't forget to point your toe in the extensions," Coach Jessica tells me in a cheery voice. She notices the exact same things as Coach Marie—I guess I really need to fix these things!

After my pattern, we warm up the jumps and spins that are in my program. My most difficult element is a loop-loop combination. A loop jump takes off backwards and is a full rotation in the air. A combination means I do one right after the other, landing on only one foot in between jumps. The first one is usually pretty easy for me, but the second one is a struggle!

"I'd like to see you check your arms in between your jumps. When I say that, I mean, don't let your arms keep swinging around you. Instead, stop your arms, keeping your left arm in front of your body. Think about hugging the circle you are skating over. This way your arms are set up to take off for your second jump."

"That makes sense. Let me try."

I skate off to try my loop-loop combination again.

"That was way easier!" I exclaim as I land it.

"It was much better. We can still make some improvements though. I'd like to see you sit more into your second jump. What I mean by that is, bend your right knee. You need a bent knee in order to spring off of it."

Coach Jessica has me stand with both knees straight and asks me to jump without bending my knees. I try but barely leave the ice.

"Okay, now bend your knees. More!" she orders as I bend them only slightly.

Once I have a really deep knee bend, she tells me to jump again.

"Which jump was higher?" she asks.

"The second."

"Why?"

"Because I bent my knees. It was much easier to jump off bent knees. I had more spring on my takeoff."

"And it's the exact same logic in the loop-loop." She smiles. "If you bend your right knee in between your jumps—and of course check your arms like we already talked about—the second jump will be much easier. Go try it again."

I skate away to try again and land the biggest loop-loop combination of my life! Wow!

"Yesss!" Coach Jessica cheers me on! "So much better, Khalli!" She gives me a fist bump, which makes me feel both proud of myself and pretty cool. I think I like her!

"All right! Let's do your program. I can't wait to see it!"

# CHAPTER 8

## *The Boy*

I talk about my lesson with Jessica the entire way home. Mom is thrilled that I'm happy and that everything has gone well. After we get home, it's time for me to get ready for today's movie with my friends. I kind of like the idea of having a big group of friends. We're going to take up half of a row at the theater!

"Becky's here!" Mom calls up the stairs, only seconds before Becky bursts through my door.

"What are you wearing? I can't decide between three different outfits—so I brought them all!"

I can't help laughing at my friend as I tell her, "You're going to be beautiful whatever you decide to wear."

"Thanks...so the blue, the green, or the purple?"

"The purple, I guess. Why?"

"Dacia's brother is dropping her off at the movies to meet us. Have you seen him lately? Just making sure he notices me. You know, so that when I'm old enough to date, I have options."

I can't help but giggle. Dacia's brother is sixteen, and he's just starting to date. Becky has had a crush on him since she was about eight, and now she's getting jealous.

"He's way too old for you!" I exclaim.

"Oh, I know. But someday, you know, maybe someday when we're both like twenty-something… I just don't want to be Dacia's dorky friend in the back of his mind."

"You already are!" I burst out. "But that's why I love you! You're fun to be around, always giggling, and you're such a sweet person. Hopefully, when you're twenty-something, if you still like him, he'll notice that about you."

"Thank you, Guidance Counselor Khalli!" Becky jokes. "But seriously, I love that you love me for who I am! Now what should I wear?"

We decide on the blue because we believe it'll look more serious and mature. Becky wants a new look for today, so we borrow my mom's hair straightener.

"I don't know why you think you need that, Becky. I would give anything for curls like yours!" Mom tries to persuade Becky to leave her hair as is.

"It's just a new look for today. Khalli already told me I'm perfect the way I am, so I guess my curls will be back again tomorrow, or whenever I wash my hair next."

Mom gives me an approving smile, letting me know she is proud of my encouragement towards Becky.

"Okay, just be careful, girls. It gets really hot," Mom warns as she passes her brand-new straightener to us.

It takes nearly forever to straighten the curls out of Becky's copper-red hair. But once her hair is straight, she looks like a totally different person.

"Who are you?" I ask in a drawn-out, questioning tone.

Becky smiles. "The new girl—just call me Rebecca."

"Weird. Nope. Not doing it!"

"Yeah, as soon as I said it, I decided it sounded wrong. I'm definitely a Becky!"

"Lip gloss?" I ask just as Mom calls up the stairs, saying Auntie Liz is here to take us to the movie theater.

"Absolutely! What do you have?"

I show her my three different shades of practically clear lip gloss, and we take our time putting it on just right. We have learned not to hurry because we know Mom and Auntie Liz are going to need at least five minutes to talk.

We sprint down the stairs out of pure excitement, and Auntie Liz stares at Becky.

"Who's the boy?" she asks immediately, her eyes twinkling at her daughter.

Becky's face turns beet red, and we both look away because we know our moms will read our faces.

"I did the same thing for a boy when I was your age, except I crimped my hair, making tiny little waves across my entire head, because that was cool at the time."

Mom and Auntie Liz bust out laughing and suddenly start talking about some boy named Ryan. Saved! Becky and I figure we can sneak away from this conversation, so we start running to the car.

"Nice try!" Auntie Liz calls as we zip past her to the car. "We'll talk on the way."

In the car, Auntie Liz asks about the boy and can't help but smile when she hears that it's Dacia's brother Danny. She reminds Becky that she's not allowed to date yet, and that when she is allowed, the boy will have to be closer to her age.

"It's just a crush, Mom!" Becky's face gets red again. "And it's not my fault. If he weren't so perfect, I wouldn't have to like him!"

Auntie Liz giggles at her daughter but then reminds Becky of the rules yet again. And then, following her mini lecture, she asks a ton of questions about Danny. Becky, of course, spills all the details!

We pull up to Keeloni's house where we are picking up Keeloni and Tanja. Dacia will meet us at the theater, maybe with her brother Danny. The rest of the ride, there is nonstop girl talk and excitement. This is the first time our moms have let us do something like this! We won't be completely alone. Auntie Liz is going to see the movie with us—but still! This is such a cool thing!

*****

At the movie theater, Dacia is waiting for us. Danny is already gone.

"He and his girlfriend are in theater number 7, he told me I could interrupt if I need anything," Dacia tells us.

"I think you need something, you should ask him to come out to the lobby," Becky giggles.

Dacia ignores her. She can't get past how gross it is that Becky thinks Danny is cute.

"So…snacks?" I announce, trying to keep everyone happy.

We buy the biggest bucket of popcorn to share. It even comes with free refills! We also each order a soda and take our cups to the soda fountain to fill.

"Let's mix flavors! We can each mix a different flavor and try each other's creations!" Becky exclaims.

I mix fruit punch with lemonade. It turns out quite fantastic! Dacia mixes fruit punch and cola—also yummy! Becky, being the crazy one, mixes lemon lime, with cola, orange, and root beer. The four of us watch her intently as she takes her first sip through the straw. Her face immediately scrunches in disgust as soon as the liquid hits her mouth.

"I don't think I can drink this," Becky stutters between gagging coughs. "It's so gross! Do you want to try?" She passes her drink to Keeloni.

"No way! You just said it was gross!" Keeloni laughs.

Next Becky passes her drink to Dacia and Tanja, who both refuse. I'm next.

"Khalli, I know you are just as weird as me on the inside, and that means you're curious about how bad this actually tastes. I think you should try."

"You're lucky you're my best friend," I joke as I reach for the cup. I take a small sip and smile. "You have offered me way grosser foods before. This is bad, but it's not nearly as nasty as your salted gummy bear cookies!"

"Your what?" Tanja looks absolutely disgusted.

"I found this delicious recipe for salted caramel cookies last summer—but we didn't have all the ingredients for the caramel. I took the obvious next best option and substituted gummy bears. They weren't that bad…" Becky looks to Dacia and me to back her up.

Dacia and I just shake our heads with big smiles on our faces. We love our crazy-fun friend—but those cookies were disgusting!

"Girls, are you ready to take your seats?" Auntie Liz asks as she comes back from the concessions counter.

"In a minute, I need to run to the bathroom first."

Becky runs off with her drink while Auntie Liz calls after her that she could hold her cup. The four of us can't help but giggle, we know Becky is really running to dump out her drink.

"Man! I need a refill—I just drank that whole thing!" Becky holds in a laugh as she refills her cup with orange and lemon lime. Auntie Liz shakes her head, now fully aware of what just happened.

"Come on, ladies! Let's go watch this movie before I change my mind about spending the next several hours with you!" Auntie Liz leads us to theater number 4, where the entire eighth row is ours!

# CHAPTER 9

## *My Hard Work Is Starting to Pay Off!*

It's Monday morning, and my project is due today. I spent all day Sunday practicing my lines. I want to be a perfect mini Surya!

I go skating before school. I had planned to wear my skating dress to the rink and then head straight to school afterwards, but Mom talked me out of it. She told me I would make more of an impact if my classmates didn't see my dress before my presentation. I agree with her, although I think she really doesn't want me to wear my dress all morning because she's afraid I'll wear it out while falling during practice.

I fall a lot when I practice. It used to bother me, but Coach Marie says falling is part of the learning process. Coach Marie also says our decision to get up and keep going makes us much stronger than someone who never falls or someone who is afraid to try new things. She has made me feel proud of my crashes! And I've learned she's right—most of my falls have eventually led to successes and new skills!

Today I do not have a lesson. I have a lesson with Coach Marie tomorrow, and I'm determined to have a perfect loop-

loop combination to show her! After my lesson with Coach Jessica, I feel like I understand exactly what I need to do to make this jump perfect every time. Now I just need to work really hard to make it a habit. Coach Marie calls this muscle memory; it basically means my brain learns how to do something so well that my body can do the skill without me thinking so much about it. I want to fix my jump combination and turn it into muscle memory!

My first couple loop-loop combinations are a little rough. I really need to think hard about what Coach Jessica told me. I make sure to check my arms after my first jump, and I work to keep my core muscles tight so I don't twist. *Bam!* A perfectly clean jump! Time to do it again. And again. And again. I land fifteen perfect loop-loop combinations.

"Way to go, Khalli!" Yana cheers me on as we meet at the rink boards for a drink of water.

"Thanks! This combo is getting a lot easier! Now I just need to land it in my program."

"Do you want to do your program now? I can play your music for you."

I hate bothering other skaters to press play at the beginning of my program, so I decide that since Yana volunteered, now is the best time. I pull up my program music on my phone and gratefully pass it to Yana.

I thank her as I skate off to strike my starting pose. Yana is waiting with her finger on the Play button. As soon as I'm in my pose, she hits Play and skates off to work on her skills. It's rare for other skaters to watch my program; they have things to work on, and standing around watching another person skate isn't one of those things.

This concept of not watching programs was difficult for me at first. I wanted to watch every program because so many of the other skaters are so amazing! Coach Marie told me I was there to skate. If I ever want to be good like the top skaters, I need to focus on my skills, not simply watch program after program during my ice time. I need to watch to make sure to stay out of the way, of course; whoever is doing their program has the right of way at the ice rink. But that's it. Sometimes I like to watch other skaters before or after my ice session, but when I'm on the ice, I'm there to skate, not to watch a show.

I push my way through my program. One minute thirty seconds doesn't sound too long, but it is when it's packed full of jumps, spins, and other difficult skills. I nail my loop-loop, which gives me a burst of energy and excitement that helps me push to the end. This was my first clean program! Every element was good! I hope I can do this again for my coaches to see!

After I finish, I quickly unplug my phone so the next skater can go and push myself for five powerful laps around the rink. Coach Marie always makes me do laps after my program. Doing laps will help me build my endurance, making me stronger, and my program will get easier the next time. As I grow as a skater, my programs will get longer. I need to prepare myself to handle a longer program, so I may as well start now!

*****

When I get to school, I don't have any time to spare before class starts. I've pushed myself to the very last minute of morning ice and had to rush to get my skates off.

We are beginning with our presentations today, but Mrs. Hill said she'd give us time to change our clothes. I am thankful for this because otherwise I would have had to leave the rink sooner, and getting the most out of every practice is so important to me. I can't wait for my classmates to see my skating dress and to tell them about Surya Bonaly!

"Good morning, everyone!" Mrs. Hill welcomes us. "After I take attendance, I will dismiss you in small groups to go to the bathroom to change. I expect you to change quickly and to be quiet in the halls. You are to go to your locker, if needed, to the bathroom, and then come directly back to the classroom. If I learn of anyone wandering the halls, it will be an automatic recess detention. Understood?"

I swear she makes eye contact with each individual student before continuing.

"While you are waiting for your turn to change and after you have returned, I expect you to be in your desk, reading over your lines silently. Today is going to be a very interesting and unique day, but I need your help to make everything run smoothly. Does anyone have any questions about what is expected of them right now?"

Nobody raises their hand, so Mrs. Hill walks over to her computer to take attendance.

"Gio, Jake, Dacia, and Sarah, you four may go change first. The rest of you may begin silently rehearsing your lines in your desks."

Mrs. Hill dismisses two boys and two girls at a time to go change into their clothes for the project. Becky and Keeloni go together in the last group. I had been really hoping to go with one of them so I could try to figure out what their big secret is. No such luck! At least I know they have a secret… The rest of my classmates have no clue!

# CHAPTER 10

## *Changing the World*

We are all sitting in our desks practicing our speeches silently, all except for Becky and Keeloni. Where are they? I can't imagine they decided to leave school when they are both so excited for this project...

"All right, ladies and gentlemen! It's time to get started! Right now you are to clear your desk except for your note card, or anything else you may need for your project, and something to write with. I am passing out a worksheet where you are expected to write two facts for each person you learn about today. I will collect this at the end."

"I expect that you will be on your best behavior today as we have a lot of famous guests! Any students causing disruptions will have consequences—and I promise, you will not like the consequences one bit." Mrs. Hill gives us all another stern look. "Are there any questions?"

I struggle with whether or not I should raise my hand and tell my teacher that Becky and Keeloni are still missing—but she has to know, right? I really don't want to upset or interrupt Mrs. Hill, but I also don't want my friends to miss anything.

Right as I'm about to raise my hand, Keeloni struts in boldly, chin high, confidence radiating from her, yet she firmly holds a solemn expression on her face. She's wearing a long, dark dress with a shawl draped over her shoulders. She has a bonnet pulled over her tiny, long, dark brown braids.

And then she begins to speak. Her voice is controlled, and her pace demonstrates intelligence, confidence, and pure honesty. She speaks with an accent that nearly sounds foreign. I see Becky step in the doorway and wait patiently.

"Well, children, where there is so much racket there must be something out of kilter. I think that twixt the Negroes of the South and the women at the North, all talking about rights, the white men will be in a fix pretty soon. But what's all this here talking about?"

Then Keeloni points at Jake.

"That man over there says that women need to be helped into carriages and lifted over ditches and to have the best place everywhere. Nobody ever helps me into carriages or over mud puddles or gives me any best place! And ain't I a woman?"

She looks down at herself, shaping her body and arms to match the expression of her voice.

"Look at me! Look at my arm! I have plowed and planted and gathered into barns, and no man could head me! And ain't I a woman? I could work as much and eat as much as a man—when I could get it—and bear the lash as well! And ain't I a woman? I have borne thirteen children, and seen most all sold off to slavery, and when I cried out with my mother's grief, none but Jesus heard me! And ain't I a woman?"

Keeloni pauses and looks up to the ceiling.

"If the first woman God ever made was strong enough to turn the world upside down all alone, these women together ought to be able to turn it back and get it right side up again! And now they is asking to do it, the men, better let them.

"Obliged to you for hearing me, and now old Sojourner ain't got nothing more to say."

Complete silence. My classmates look around at each other—nobody is entirely sure what just happened. Keeloni's speech was so powerful! But who is she?

Becky steps forward into the room. Her outfit is similar to that of Keeloni, except her dress has a lot more detail. It looks like a more expensive version of Keeloni's dress, like she's a wealthier woman in the same time period. Her red curls are pinned back and tucked mostly behind her head; her chin is held high. Actually, I don't think she could sink her chin if she wanted to. Her neck is wrapped tightly in a rippled collar; it almost reminds me of a coffee filter. She looks like a doll!

"Sojourner, Sojourner Truth! What a pleasure to have you with us today!" Becky greets Keeloni.

"I am so honored to get to talk to all of you fine people," Keeloni continues in her unique accent. "And it's such a pleasure to be here with you today. Ladies and gentlemen, please welcome a woman who believes as I do, Harriet Beecher Stowe!"

My classmates and I automatically applaud. It's like Keeloni and Becky are actually Sojourner Truth and Harriet Beecher Stowe! Their presentation is so good...and they're just getting started!

"Sojourner, it has been such an honor to work towards the same goals with you: the goals of human rights and the goals of abolition—which is the goal to end slavery. I would love for you to share more about your life with these fine people." Becky swoops her arm across the classroom, letting us all know that we are the fine people who are about to be told a great story.

"It would be my honor," Keeloni smiles.

"My name is Sojourner Truth, but that wasn't always my name. I was born as Isabella Baumfree in 1797 in New York. I was born into slavery. My owner, I guess we will call him, died when I was nine, and my family was split up and sold at auctions. I was sold with a flock of sheep for one hundred dollars. Can you believe that? One hundred dollars—that's all they believed my life was worth! I was sold three more times over the next several years. During this time, I learned English. Until I was removed from my first owner, my family and I only spoke Dutch—this is why I have a bit of an accent.

"I was usually not treated well. Some owners beat me, some harassed me, none of them loved me. I was property.

"With my husband, I gave birth to five children. My youngest son died as a child—he never saw freedom. In 1826,

I walked into freedom with my infant daughter. I could not take my other children with me. You see, New York had started to free slaves, but my older children were not to be free until they had worked long enough to earn their freedom.

"I found a family, the Van Wagenens, who offered to let me live with them. They bought my services and paid my prior owner because I was not yet fully free. It was then that I learned my five-year-old son had been sold illegally to a slaveholder in the South. With the help of the Van Wagenen family, I formed a court case and fought! Imagine me, a black woman, once a slave, taking a white man to court…but I did!

"And I won!" A bold smile spreads across Keeloni's face. "I was the first African American woman in the United States to win a lawsuit in court.

"I also became a devout Christian. I started taking an interest in helping the poor and made many other devout Christian friends. As my faith grew, I changed my name from Isabella Baumfree to Sojourner Truth. The spirit had called me, it was time to act.

"I began travelling and preaching about the end of slavery. I didn't want people to live the way I had. I didn't want people to be beaten, to have their children beaten and sold. I wanted everyone to have freedom.

"I advocated for both women and African Americans, which was very dangerous for me, especially because I was both. I travelled the country, preaching what I believed, preaching for rights. During my travels, I met many people who held the same beliefs as me. These people helped me to believe that there was hope. One of these people is here with us today! Please welcome… Harriet Beecher Stowe!"

The entire class claps and cheers—it's like we are at a real human rights rally!

"Harriet, would you be willing to tell these fine people about your life?" Keeloni asks, turning to Becky.

"Absolutely!" Becky smiles. "My story is unique, although my past isn't as difficult as yours. But it is the pasts of people like you that have inspired me to make a difference."

Becky turns to my classmates to tell the story of Harriet Beecher Stowe.

"I was born in 1811 to a very religious family. My father was a preacher, and my mother, who died when I was five, also trusted greatly in God. I believe it is safe to say that my upbringing guided me to fight for equality and human rights.

"I attended school at a female seminary run by my older sister. I was quite thankful for this opportunity as quality education for girls was very rare in the 1800s. When I was in my early twenties, I moved from my home in Connecticut to Ohio with my dad. Living in Ohio opened my eyes to the injustices between races.

"There were riots in Cincinnati, the city where I lived. These riots were against African Americans because other people feared the black people were taking their jobs. I met with many of the African Americans who suffered the riots, they taught me so much and really opened my eyes to racial injustices as well as slavery.

"I met my husband in Ohio, he also disagreed with slavery. Together we supported the Underground Railroad. This is not a real railroad but a network of secret routes and safe houses that was used to help slaves escape to freedom!

"My husband and I moved back East, and it was here that I had a vision during a communion service at church. My vision was of a dying slave—and I decided to write his story.

"This story became known as the famous *Uncle Tom's Cabin*. With this book I hoped to educate Northerners about the pain, suffering, and horrors caused by slavery. I wanted people of the North to understand what was really happening in the South, and I wanted people in the south to understand the feelings of the people they were forcing into slavery. It has even been suggested that this book played an impact in the beginning of the American Civil War. The truth of that, I will never know.

"I wrote many articles and books, including an article on Sojourner." Becky gestures across the room towards Keeloni.

"I took some liberty to adjust some of the facts about your life, and for that I am sorry. But please understand, Sojourner, I did so with intent to make my readers more empathetic to the struggles of black people in America."

Keeloni steps forward again. "I understand, and I thank you for your support. There have been a lot of good white people who have helped change the fate of African Americans, who have helped us break free from the chains of slavery. And as a woman, it has been an honor to work aside other women who also had limited rights but who continued to fight for more."

Becky nods her head. "I feel the same. I think about the struggles and injustices I faced as a white woman, and I understand that I cannot truly grasp how much more difficulty you faced as a black woman. I thank you for spreading your truth and your story."

"And I thank you for listening…and for truly hearing my story." Keeloni acknowledges both Becky and all of our classmates.

The two girls grab hands and raise their arms together for a bow.

My classmates and I look at each other. Wow! What a message! But who wants to present after that? It was so good! I definitely do not want to go next.

"Let's give Keeloni and Becky—or should I say, Sojourner Truth and Harriet Beecher Stowe—a round of applause!" Mrs. Hill steps forward from her seat behind all of us.

I had forgotten she was sitting back there; I was so focused on the presentation.

The class begins clapping, and then Gio stands up. Along with Gio, Tanja and Dacia join; so do I. Soon the entire class is giving a standing ovation in recognition, not only of Keeloni's and Becky's hard work, but also in recognition of these two women who helped change the course of the world.*

---

* Sources:

"Ain't I a Woman?" by Sojourner Truth, www.feminist.com/resources/artspeech/genwom/sojour.htm.

# CHAPTER 11

## *Heroes*

"Keeloni, Becky, thank you! Your presentation was fantastic and so full of information—well done! Everyone else, please make sure you have two facts written down on your worksheet for Sojourner Truth and two facts written down for Harriet Beecher Stowe."

Shoot! I totally forgot to fill out the worksheet during the presentation!

"I see a lot of you scrambling to fill in your worksheet," Mrs. Hill announces, "so let's take a couple minutes to write, and then we will go on to our next presentation. Are there any volunteers?"

Nobody raises their hand. I imagine everyone is thinking that after how well Becky and Keeloni did, they don't want to follow.

---

Sojourner Truth: The Libyan Sibyl, docsouth.unc.edu/highlights/sojournertruth.html.

History.com Editors. (2009, November 12). Harriet Beecher Stowe. https://www.history.com/topics/american-civil-war/harriet-beecher-stowe

Harriet Beecher Stowe. Miss rich: Civil War. (n.d.). https://sites.google.com/site/missrichcivilwar/m-abolitionist-leaders/harriet-beecher-stowe

Mrs. Hill waits patiently while we all write as fast as we can.

"Last chance for volunteers before I choose who will go next," Mrs. Hill tells us calmly.

Dacia raises her hand. "I'll go."

Dacia really doesn't like public speaking, so I imagine she just wants to get it over with.

Dacia approaches the front of the class. Her straight, dark hair is pulled back off her face and into a low ponytail. She's wearing a long navy dress with ribbon-like seams. Around her neck, she has a stole, like the colorful sashes people often wear at graduation. She looks important, whoever she is.

"Ladies and gentlemen, hello. I am Marie Curie," Dacia begins. She tells us she was born in Warsaw, Poland, in 1867 and eventually studied physics in Paris, France. She received half a Nobel Prize in physics, which she shared with her husband for their work on radioactivity and later received a second Nobel Prize, this time in chemistry, for her studies on radium. In addition to her two Nobel Prizes, she earned many other awards, proving that as a woman, she could also be a scientist.

I can tell Dacia is nervous as she talks, but it's also obvious she's determined to do a good job and has prepared more than enough to beat her nerves. Doing a school presentation is kind of like taking a skating test. You know going into it that you're going to be nervous, but you also know that if you prepare like crazy, you will be ready to conquer the nerves. I can't believe how much figure skating is teaching me about life!

I jot down my two facts about Marie Curie as Dacia presents and give her a thumbs-up as she finishes. She smiles at me, clearly grateful that I appreciated her presentation.

Tanja volunteers to go next. Wearing a nearly all white robe with blue stripes across the head cloth, she introduces herself as Mother Teresa, or Saint Teresa of Calcutta.

"I was born in what is modern-day Macedonia in 1910. When I was twelve already, I felt I had a calling from God to become a missionary, and when I was eighteen, I left my parents to join a community of nuns."

Tanja tells our class how Mother Teresa worked as a teacher and how she was impacted by the suffering she saw outside of the convent walls. After about fifteen years as a teacher, Mother Teresa left the convent to work in the slums of Calcutta, India. Here she started a school in the open air for children. She also created an organization that aimed to love and care for people that nobody else was prepared to care for.

"I, Mother Teresa, devoted my entire life to making the world a better place. I showed love to people who hadn't felt love and cared for people when nobody else would. I left such an impact that after my death, the Catholic Church made me a saint."

The class claps for Tanja, and I suddenly realize that I'm the last of my friends to present. Maybe I should go right away and get it done with. Immediately my palms begin to sweat, and my stomach is swarming with nerves. If I don't go now, these nerves may not go away. I raise my hand; I have to get this over with—and now! Just as my hand reaches its full extension in the air, I hear Mrs. Hill.

"Yes, Gio. Thank you for raising your hand so calmly. It would be our pleasure to watch your presentation. And, Khalli, you may go after Gio."

After Gio? Now I can't even change my mind! I wanted to go right now, but now I have to sit here and think about my presentation the entire time Gio is presenting because I'm definitely next. How am I going to hear a word he says?

Gio struts boldly to the front of the room. "Hey, everyone! I'm Joe Louis, you know, the boxer."

That explains why he's wearing a robe over his gym shorts and tank top. I like that he picked an athlete too. Two athletes, one right after the other… Oh shoot… I'm next!

"I am a very strong black man, as you can see." Gio flexes his arms for our class. "But I was born in 1914, a time when being black was incredibly difficult. As a boxer, my job was often to fight in the ring against white men. I like to work hard, and I like to win. I usually win." Gio smiles. "But in my career, I was often winning against white men, that's kind of scary for a black man who was thought to be lesser by society. But I knew my role, and I presented myself honorably. When I won, I didn't gloat. And I won a lot. I was the heavyweight champion of the world from 1937 to 1949. I became admired by Americans of all colors—me, a black man."

Gio goes on to tell about the humility of Joe Louis, about his role in society and in the ring.

"My first professional loss was to a German, Max Schmeling, in 1936. This was the era when Adolf Hitler was ruling Germany. I got to rematch Schmeling in 1938. I felt so much pressure. Because Schmeling was from Germany, and the Nazis ruling Germany were causing so much pain, the media made it seem like our boxing match was actually a battle between democracy, which is the American way of government, and Nazism. The American media also made a point about me, a black man, fighting against a white German. Schmeling wasn't a Nazi, but his ruler Adolf Hitler was in the process of eliminating anyone who wasn't his ideal race… white. In Germany, I would have been eliminated. I had to win, democracy had to win! And I did!"

Wow! Another presentation that teaches our class about the impact an athlete can make, right before my presentation on Surya Bonaly. Joe Louis was also a black athlete in his sport during a time where this wasn't the norm. This will actually be a great transition! I wonder if Mrs. Hill thought about this when she chose Gio to go right before me…

Gio wraps up his presentation about the incredible boxer Joe Louis by talking about his return to the boxing ring after retirement due to his struggles with money, his impact on the sport, on society, and ends by telling about all of his awards, including an induction into the International Boxing Hall of Fame in 1990.

I find I am quite impressed.

"Khalli, are you ready? I would love for the class to hear about another incredibly talented and hardworking athlete, this time representing France."

I can't really tell Mrs. Hill that I'm not ready, so I guess it's now or never.

I slowly rise from my desk and strut as confidently as possible to the front of the room. I am wearing my beautiful skating dress, the one Mom and Dad bought me right before my test last month. It's this perfect mix of purples and blues, with wisps of other colors and crystals…and pure magic! The deep purple and magenta at the top melt into a bold blue at the waist, which then fades into a lighter blue with wisps of green swirled into the skirt. It's covered in crystals and makes me feel like a champion just by putting it on—I can hardly wait to compete in this dress!

Surya Bonaly always had beautiful, bold dresses too. At first they were homemade by her mom, but as her fame grew, her dresses were actually created by famous designers with Surya's input—designers like Christian Lacroix. None of her dresses looked quite like mine, but I imagine she felt just as amazing in her skating dresses as I do when I wear mine!

I reach the front of the room. Glancing at my classmates, I immediately feel all of my nerves kick into full effect.

I suddenly hear the words of Coach Marie in my head—the words she encouraged me with right before my very first skating test last month. *"You've worked so incredibly hard for this. Now go get it!"*

I've worked really hard on this presentation, just like I did on my skating test. I stayed in for so many recesses working. I put in lots of time at home. I practiced my speech in front of my parents several times. I'm prepared. I need to focus and nail this—just like I would a skating test!

"*Je m'appelle Surya Bonaly*," I introduce myself and tell my classmates what this means. Then I continue. "I was born in France, in 1973, and originally named Claudine, but my parents changed my name to Surya when they adopted me at eight months old. *Surya* means 'goddess of the sun' in the Indian language.

"My process to become an Olympian started later than most. I didn't begin as a figure skater when I was young. Instead I actually participated in a variety of sports—I always worked hard, and as a result, I found I was good at them all. I dedicated years of my life to gymnastics and tumbling as a child and became the Junior World Champion at age twelve! This later helped me to become a stronger skater.

"I started training more intensively in figure skating when I was ten years old, and I moved to Paris shortly after this to train with Didier Gailhaguet. Already, as a child, I gave up so many social opportunities in order to pursue my skating goal. I didn't have time for birthday parties, sleepovers, or hanging out with friends on the weekends—if I was going to achieve my dream, I needed to train. I even moved hours away from my home to train with my new coach. Because I started skating a bit older than most elite skaters, I had work to do in order to catch up—and you best believe I worked!

I worked so hard that after a year with my new coach, I was already on the French National team.

"By age twelve I was combining my gymnastic abilities with my skating, and through lots of effort, I learned how to do a backflip on ice! This trick would eventually turn into one of my signature moves. To make the backflip along with all my other skills possible, I put in more time than most people can even imagine. Hours upon hours daily; those hours turned to years, which turned to decades of dedication to my sport. I gave up a lot in trade for my success in figure skating and suffered many injuries—including completely shredding my Achilles tendon. But through all of my effort and struggles, I never gave up my love for the ice!"

I tell my class about all of Surya's medals and awards—how she competed all over the world and was the only woman ever to land a backflip on one foot in a competition! And then I tell my class about how Surya was different from what the figure skating world was used to. Her moves were sharp and powerful. With every ounce of her energy, Surya aimed to radiate positivity and happiness on the ice through her creative movements, and because of her athleticism, she was able to achieve flawlessly exquisite positions that many can only dream of—and she made them look easy!

"I was strong, I was consistent, I was powerful...and I am black."

Through my presentation, my classmates learn about how Surya stood out as the only elite skater of color during most of her competitive years.

"I was a pioneer for future generations of skaters, but I didn't even know it at the time."

I talk about how Surya's success both opened the door for, and inspired, skaters of all colors, incredible skaters like my friend Yana. I tell about her involvement promoting figure skating with African American girls in Harlem and other areas. What an inspiration!

"Because of my hard work and achievements, people know about me. I can use my fame to make a difference in the world. And I do, still today. I continue to fight for what I believe is right, for people, for animals, and for fairness and equality."

Finally, I teach my classmates how, after her competitive career, Surya went on to skate professionally around the world and how the audiences cheered for her and her bold style of skating. Through every performance, Surya gained the love and admiration of the crowd worldwide.

"I was fully appreciated for my skating style. I could shine by being exactly who I am! Because of the awe I inspired in my audience, I am well-known across the globe even years after my last performance. My longevity in the skating world is monumental, a firm testament to my dedication. So please use me as an example. I am no different than you—I started something new as a beginner, worked extremely hard, and my hard work paid off. With enough effort, your work will create amazing results too." And then I wrap up my presentation with a little more French that I learned from Yana.

"And with that, I would like to close by saying thank you very much and goodbye. So…*merci beaucoup et au revoir*."

My class applauds, and I walk happily back to my desk, knowing that my preparation and hard work led to a great performance, this time for my classmates.

"Thank you, Khalli. *Merci*!" Mrs. Hill steps to the front of the room.

Gio shoots up his hand, and Mrs. Hill calls on him.

"So far, almost everyone else picked a role model that looked like themselves, but you didn't—I think that's cool. Why did you decide to pick Surya?"

This is an answer I don't even need to think about. "I picked Surya Bonaly because she's a figure skater like me, and her skating impressed me so much. I was in awe after the first video I watched of her. Her triple jumps are so powerful, and her backflips are the most amazing thing I've ever seen on skates! I hope that someday I can maybe achieve what she has."

Gio nods, satisfied, but I decide I should say more.

"What I didn't realize at first when I started this presentation was that her skating career was probably more difficult due to the color of her skin. I chose not to talk about her losses in my presentation, because her success goes so far beyond that. But I imagine the color of her skin required Surya to prove herself more than her competitors at times. I'm white, and therefore, I will never be in her shoes to fully understand. And because of this, I learned that it's important that we are aware that not everyone is treated the same and that we do our best to listen to others, to fix the unfairness, and to accept others."

"Khalli, those are wise words beyond your years! I think it's safe to say you taught the class not only about the incredible talent and dedication of Surya Bonaly in your presentation, but also, just now you taught us about social inequities—or the lack of fairness in our world. There have been some really good presentations today, showing me that many of you understand this. I think it's fair to say that in addition to these role models, you have each shared with us, this classroom is also full of world-changers. I couldn't be more proud of my students right now and cannot wait to see how you all make the world a better place."

We continue with our presentations, learning about a lot of people that I've heard about but didn't know why they were important—people like Ronald Reagan, Andy Warhol, Helen Keller, Nelson Mandela, Valentina Tereshkova, Barack Obama, Winston Churchill, and Mahatma Gandhi. What a wide array of heroes! It's cool for me to see what makes a hero for each of my classmates—we all chose different people for different reasons. And yet we are all right; everyone we chose truly made a difference in this world!*

---

* Sources:

"The Nobel Prize in Physics 1903." (n.d.). https://www.nobelprize.org/nobel_prizes/physics/laureates/1903/marie-curie-bio.html

"The Nobel Peace Prize 1979," *NobelPrize.org*, www.nobelprize.org/nobel_prizes/peace/laureates/1979/teresa-bio.html.

"Joe Louis," *Encyclopedia Britannica*, Encyclopedia Britannica Inc., www.britannica.com/biography/Joe-Louis.

Bonaly, Surya. Interview, conducted by Allye Ritt, December 2020.

# CHAPTER 12

## *Good Things Are Happening*

After school Auntie Liz pulls up in her beige minivan, or her mom-mobile, as she calls it.

"Hey, girls!" she calls through her partially rolled-down window. "I know it's cold out, but I had a craving for ice cream. Want to come with me to Snowtop Cream Shop… or would you rather walk home in this dreary, cold, wintry weather?" She draws out the words *dreary* and *cold* as much as possible.

"I've already asked your mom, Khalli."

Becky and I look at each other.

"Duh! Of course!" we both practically shout at the same time.

I love that my mom and Becky's mom are best friends—it makes our friendship so convenient. If it were anyone else's mom, I'd have to call home and get permission first, not with Auntie Liz though!

Once Becky and I hop into the mom-mobile, Auntie Liz changes the radio station. She's usually jamming, as she likes to call it, to '90s pop music.

"101.1, just for my two favorite ladies!" she announces as she puts on our favorite radio station.

"Why do I feel like we are celebrating something?" Becky asks with confusion.

"Because we are. We are celebrating your friendship," Auntie Liz tells us. "You two just had a big project, and your friendship was put to the test when Becky teamed up with Keeloni. Krista and I were so impressed with how maturely you two girls worked through this, and we want to show you how supportive we are of your friendship and your growing maturity. Krista is actually on her way to join us for ice cream because we really want you to know how proud we are of you both!"

"Yay! Auntie Krista!" Becky cheers and smiles at me. "I feel like I haven't seen your mom in days!"

"I know! We've been so busy on this project we haven't been to each other's houses all that much lately. This is great that we get to hang out right now!" I say with a bold smile.

"And…" Auntie Liz cuts in, "I get to see my best friend for ice cream too!"

We all laugh. It's weird thinking about how long my mom and Auntie Liz have known each other. They've been friends for over thirty years. I hope Becky and I are friends forever too!

*****

It's 5:30 a.m. and I am at the rink and ready to go. My Tuesday lessons start at 5:45 a.m. This used to seem early, but now I am determined to be warmed up and to have landed at least five loop-loop combinations before Coach Marie is ready for me.

When I look around the rink, I see only the most determined skaters. Yana, Stacy, and Tamerah are here every day early. A couple other skaters come in once or twice during the week for lessons or ice. Today Thomas is here. Normally when he's at the rink, he is pounding out jump after jump, but today he is skating around with Stacy. They are working together with Coach Marie and doing a ton of stroking exercises. I wonder if they are going to try to ice dance together. He's much bigger than Stacy, but somehow they seem to skate well together.

"They are fun to watch, aren't they?" Yana notices my interest as she begins stretching next to me at the boards. "They're going to try skating pairs together. Even though Thomas works with Damien Peters normally, he and Damien have connected with Coach Marie to find a fitting partner. Thomas and Stacy are nearly the same level, and Stacy is the perfect size. Plus, she's strong."

"Pairs? Like lifts and throws?" I ask.

"That's the plan. But that's literally all I know. Stacy just filled me in this morning. This is partner trial number 1."

"That's so cool!" *Maybe I can do pairs someday*, I think to myself as I skate off to run through parts of my program.

I just need to practice the steps going into the loop-loop. I want to feel comfortable doing it in my program, and I want to be ready for Coach Marie.

I glance at the clock, 5:43 a.m. Coach Marie will be here in two minutes. She is always perfectly on time, never more than a minute late as she runs from one student to the next, often even connecting with parents in between. I don't know how she does it!

I can still get in a couple more combos before my lesson. One clean combo jump after another! I can't wait to show my coach!

"Good morning, Khalli! I love that you're getting here earlier and earlier to skate. Soon you'll be waiting for me to unlock the door!" my coach jokes.

"I don't know about that—don't you open the rink at 4:15?"

Coach Marie nods. "I see your combos are looking better. Are you up for a full run-through of your program right away? The ice show is only a week and a half away, so I'd really like to run your program with music first."

"I'm ready," I say confidently.

My coach finds my music on her phone as I skate to my starting position.

My entry position, which used to be so difficult, is now pretty easy. I work to stretch through my body and through my core, aiming to look as tall and elongated as possible.

My first jump—a single salchow. Easy. *Hold the landing*, I tell myself. One. Two. Three. Coach Marie always makes me hold my landings to the count of three. She says if I'm going to work so hard doing my jump, then I really need to present it to let everyone know that it was an important element.

My first spin is a sit spin. It's getting better and definitely is getting lower. I can't wait to show it off in the ice show! And then the loop-loop. Perfect!

"Wooooooo!" I hear Coach Marie cheering. I did it!

I return my focus back to my program. It's worthless for me to land the loop-loop to show my coach if I'm going to mess something else up.

I strike my ending pose after a crazy-fast scratch spin.

"That's the best run-through I've ever seen you do! Very well done, Khalli. Very good!" Coach Marie gives me the biggest high five possible.

"You are ready for the ice show and for the competition in two and a half weeks! I love your efforts and hard work! Now, there are two tiny spots where I want to clean up your arms, and then we are going to work on your Lutz jump. This is the last single before the Axel," she says with a wink.

I smile proudly. I love making progress. It is worth every early morning, every scratch and bruise, and every ounce of hard work!

# CHAPTER 13

## *Don't Bail!*

It's Wednesday after school, and I have a lesson with Coach Jessica. Because she's only working with a couple students, she has openings throughout the day, rather than just super early in the mornings. I love skating before school because the ice has fewer people, but I also really enjoyed being able to sleep in today and wake up just in time to walk to school with Becky. It was refreshing. Mom, of course, said she liked it too.

I am scheduled to have three lessons with Coach Jessica this week. Since she's only here for the week of her spring break, Mom said we were going to take advantage of the opportunity to work with her. She'll be back next weekend again for the ice show because she's the guest skater. How cool that I get to be coached by the guest skater! And she'll be able to cheer me on for my very first big performance.

"Hey, Khalli! It's great to see you again! Coach Marie said you nailed your program yesterday, loop-loop included!" Coach Jessica doesn't stop smiling the entire time she's talking. "And Coach Marie told me you just started Lutz jumps yesterday. She asked me to help you with them today. Have you already warmed up your jumps enough to do them?"

I nod.

"Perfect! Do you want to go over anything first, or do you want to show me one?"

"I'll show you. I tried a couple today already, but I can't get onto the outside edge for the takeoff like Coach Marie wants. She gave me a lot of tips yesterday, but I feel like I'm forgetting some of them."

"Why don't you show me, and then we can go from there."

I skate clockwise around the ice doing backwards crossovers and glide backwards on my left foot into the corner, just like Coach Marie showed me yesterday. I pass my right arm along my body and reach it behind me. My right leg reaches back, and I drive my toe pick into the ice. And up! I land on my right leg like I'm supposed to and glance down at my tracing on the ice. Coach Marie taught me how to read my marks on the ice so I know if I am using the proper edge. Ugh! It was an inside edge; it should be an outside edge.

"Hey! Not bad, Khalli! We can definitely work with that! With a few minor adjustments, you'll be taking off clean in no time!"

I guess it's fair to say that Coach Jessica noticed I was on the wrong edge. I wonder how obvious it actually is to a coach or judge…

"Let's do the Lutz on a hockey circle." Coach Jessica shows me how to set up on the circle. "This way you can tell easily if you are changing edges—your goal is to follow the curve of the circle. Next, I want to adjust your right arm."

My coach has me stand still as she guides me into the position she wants me in. The Lutz takes off the left back outside edge; my right leg should be reaching behind me because the jump takes off of a toe pick. Skaters create outside edges by leaning the outside of their skating foot towards the ice; inside edges are when the skater leans the inside of their foot to the ice. I've learned there's a lot more technique than just this to creating good edges. I'm working hard on it, but my coaches have said this skill takes time.

"Your right arm is key. I want you to feel a little pinch right here." She presses her hand lightly behind my shoulder. "You'll achieve this by opening your shoulder."

Coach Jessica immediately realizes I have no idea what she means.

"Basically, if you roll your arm so your right thumb is pointing upwards when your arm is behind you, you'll be opening your shoulder. Just try it standing here."

I do as she asks, and suddenly what she's telling me clicks. I feel my shoulder open, and I feel the pinch just behind my shoulder blade.

"I get it. Can I try in my jump now?" I ask determined.

"Let's do that one more time while standing here, just to make sure you're comfortable with the arm."

I reach back and show Coach Jessica I understand.

"You got it! Let's see that Lutz now!"

I take off with a little more speed than usual. I am so ready to nail this jump! Setting up my edge, I reach back. Right leg and right arm back, right thumb up. And up! This jump is huge! Oh no! It's too big! I try to stop the jump mid-air, but it's too late. *Thud*!

I crash belly-first onto the ice, barely breaking my fall with my elbows and knees, yet enough that they throb just as badly as my stomach.

"Khalli! Are you okay?" Coach Jessica rushes over to me lying on the ice. She gets down on her knees when she realizes I'm not bouncing back up like I normally do.

"I'm okay," I manage to wince through my gritted teeth. "It. Just. Really hurts."

I slowly pull myself up off the ice as I fight to hold back tears. This was a tough one—perhaps one of my worst falls yet.

"Let's skate to the boards and sit for a minute. When you're ready, I want to talk about what went wrong with that jump."

"I don't want to sit. I want to fix it. Can you tell me what was wrong now? I want to do it again." I struggle to pace the words out as I fight back tears.

"Seriously?" Coach Jessica asks, her voice laced with confusion.

I nod. "I'm ready now."

My coach shakes her head in disbelief. "Marie wasn't kidding about you. You're on a mission."

I try to smile, but everything hurts. I just need to know what went wrong. Hopefully then I can fix it.

"Okay. If you're ready," Coach Jessica starts with hesitation.

"I'm ready," I repeat with as much confidence as I can muster.

"Your takeoff was great. You had a lot of height!"

"But then?"

"In the air you need to pull your weight over your right side. You've been doing this all afternoon, but this last time you dropped your left hip. Then you opened up your arms and basically flailed everything, this stopped your rotation. Once you're in the air, you really need to commit. You know how to fall from a jump, you do not know how to bail from a jump, and that's exactly what you did. Never bail midair, it will almost always end badly. Even with your weight not correctly over your right side, you probably could have finished your rotation. It would have been messy, but it would have been safer, a lot safer."

"I kind of freaked out when I was in the air. I'm not used to jumps that big."

"It was huge!" Coach Jessica says with the first smile since I crashed.

"Okay. I understand. I'm going to do it again."

Coach Jessica opens her mouth to object, but I turn and skate off before she can say anything to stop me. I want to land this jump so badly. I want to start my Axel.

I skate a little more slowly than last time. That fall really hurt, and I definitely don't want to do it again. Ever again. I'm going to commit to this jump.

On my left back outside edge, I reach back. *Thumb up*, I tell myself. *Pick, lift, stay over the right side. And land.* Smooth sailing! I glance down at my tracing on the ice—a clean outside edge!

"Yes! Khalli, that was it! You just landed a clean Lutz!"

I beam back at Coach Jessica. I cannot wait to start my Axel!

# CHAPTER 14

## *The Axel Is Coming*

On Thursday, I didn't have a lesson, but I went skating so I could practice. Now that I've landed a couple clean Lutz jumps, I'm determined to land more. Friday, I worked with Coach Jessica again for my final lesson. I won't work with her again until she comes home next weekend for the ice show. Today is Saturday, and I have a lesson with Coach Marie—I can't wait to show her my Lutz!

"Can we start with my Lutz jump?" I ask immediately when Coach Marie skates over to me.

"Hi Khalli, nice to see you too," my coach jokes.

I smile back at her. I am so excited to show her my progress that I guess I forgot to greet her. Oops!

"And yes, we can. And then we are going to work on your program. The ice show is next weekend already, and then your first competition is the following week. I want to make sure you feel ready."

"Okay. I'm warmed up. Can I just go and do it?" I can hardly contain my excitement.

Coach Marie nods calmly. I wish she were more excited.

I skate off and set up my jump. As I do my backwards crossovers, I think about all of the things Coach Jessica helped me work through. I reach back and totally nail the landing!

"Khalli! That is so much better!"

There's the excitement I was hoping for!

"You've fixed your takeoff edge, and your air position is much cleaner. Jessica told me you worked on it, but I didn't expect that much progress! I should know never to question your potential, shouldn't I?"

I smile shyly. I love making my coach happy.

"I just want to make one minor adjustment, and that's where your head is looking."

Coach Marie helps me straighten out my head position, and I attempt and cleanly land three more, one after another.

"Khalli, this Lutz is so good that after this competition, it might be time to put it in your program! And then, Axels are coming," she says with a wink.

I can hardly wait to start my Axel! It is literally making me crazy with excitement.

"Let's do your program." Coach Marie never wastes any time.

I skate to my starting position as she waits to press Play. Soon enough I'll be putting the Lutz and other big jumps into this program!

*****

After skating, I have plans with Becky and Dacia. We are going to the mall. Spring break is only a week away at our school. Both Becky and Dacia are going on vacation and want new outfits. I wish my parents would take me somewhere for the week.

"Where are you guys even going that you need new clothes?" I ask as soon as we meet up at the food court.

Becky and Dacia rode together with Auntie Liz, who will be staying with us at the mall. My mom dropped me off right after I finished at the rink. She even gave me fifteen dollars.

"For lunch, and spend whatever is left," she told me with a tired smile.

"My family is going to Florida. My grandparents are there for the winter, so we are going to visit and will stay at their house all week. I can't wait to see them!" Becky tells us excitedly.

"Where are you going, Dacia?"

"I am leaving the country," Dacia tells us proudly and matter-of-factly.

"What? Where are you going?" Becky asks, clearly a little jealous.

"We are going to Vietnam to see family. My aunt and uncle still live there, and my dad says he misses his brother and wants us to meet him. I have little cousins there too. My dad usually goes back home every year or so, but this is the first time we all get to go with him. I'm so excited, but also a little nervous. I don't speak a lot of Vietnamese."

"Does your brother speak the language?" I ask.

"Danny speaks better than I do. He was born there, and when my parents first moved to America, they spoke only Vietnamese at home. They started using more English at home because they wanted Danny and me to speak fluent English. They said that since I'm an American-born citizen, it's important my English is strong. Mom, Dad, and Danny are all US citizens now too."

"I always forget that your family isn't from here…well, until I eat your mom's food. She makes the best pho soup ever!" Becky giggles.

"So true!" I agree. "So what are you both shopping for?" I try to change the subject. I'm bummed that I don't have a vacation to talk about.

"I need summer clothes. I outgrew my shorts from last year. And a new swimsuit. Maybe you can help me pick out one your brother might like?" Becky jokes with Dacia.

"Eeew! No way!" Dacia exclaims. "You're gross!"

I guess even what we are shopping for is going to bring our conversation right back to vacation. I decide when I get the chance, I'm going to ask my parents about taking a vacation.

"All right, girls!" Auntie Liz comes back to our table with a smoothie in hand. "Where are we shopping first?"

"At stores with ugly swimsuits," Dacia announces matter-of-factly.

"Don't ask…" Becky gives her mom a look, suggesting that Dacia is just a little crazy.

I giggle to myself. Today will be fun, even if I don't have a reason to shop.

# CHAPTER 15

## *Pancakes and Sacrifices*

Sunday is family day. Sometimes I get to skate, but as much as possible, my parents try to plan things that we can all do together.

Our Sunday mornings always start off at church. First Sunday school and then the service. I used to think church was too early on a day off. But now that I have skating before school, sleeping in until 8:00 a.m. seems nearly impossible. Sunday school at 9:00 a.m. doesn't seem early at all anymore.

My dad teaches Sunday school, so he takes me to church with him; my mom meets us in time for the service.

"Where's Mom?" I ask at breakfast.

"Your mom has been waking up so early to get you to the rink all week, I told her she should sleep and I'd make you breakfast," my dad tells me.

"I'm sure she liked that idea. So what did you make me for breakfast?"

Normally Mom has eggs and bacon or pancakes all ready for me when I come downstairs.

"Cereal," Dad says with a twinkle in his eye.

"Seriously?"

"Yep. And I even cut up fresh strawberries for you to add to your cornflakes so that your bowl looks just like the cover of the cereal box. I know, gourmet, right? I impress myself as well!"

I try really hard not to laugh at Dad and to show my disappointment of my Sunday breakfast. Normally Sunday breakfast is the best. I fail. I can't hold my smirk back, and Dad knows he's off the hook.

"Thanks, Dad."

"Wait, there's more." Dad hands me a Styrofoam bowl and plastic spoon. "Pure class."

"Okay, you're definitely kidding now, right?"

"Nope. It's like camping, right here in our kitchen. And the best part, no dishes for Mom when she wakes up. Just don't tell her I fed you cereal, okay?"

"Ha! I'm totally telling her!"

"I knew you would. I can't get away with anything, can I?"

I eat my "gourmet" cereal quickly and hurry off to Sunday school.

*****

After church Mom and Dad have a surprise planned for lunch.

"Since I ruined breakfast," Dad begins, "we are going to have pancakes for lunch! But not just any pancakes…"

We stop at the grocery store, and Dad takes me into the cake-decorating aisle.

"Pick out what you want for decorating. I expect these pancakes to be beautiful!"

I pick out rainbow sprinkles and two types of icing, in pink and green. I've never decorated pancakes before!

"Mark? Khalli? How much sugar are you two buying?" Mom asks in astonishment when she turns the corner into the aisle, arms full of fresh fruits and vegetables.

"Don't look at me, Krista. Your daughter picked this out…with maybe a little encouragement from her father…," Dad responds with a gaping smile.

Mom shakes her head but quickly accepts defeat. "Okay, but only if I get to help decorate!"

At home, Dad and I make the pancakes together. We even add food coloring to the mix to make different-colored pancakes—yellow, blue, green pancakes, and some pancakes with swirls of colors mixed together.

"These look disgusting!" Mom jokes.

"Don't worry, they are definitely going to taste deliciously unhealthy!" Dad replies.

"Can you two put some blueberries in mine? At least I'll have some nutritional value for the afternoon then," Mom requests.

That's a great idea! I decide to put blueberries in the rest of the pancakes. I should probably eat the blueberry pancakes too. Healthier food gives me more energy, and energy is key in skating!

Once the pancakes are made, we all sit down at the table and decorate together. I choose a blue blueberry pancake and draw a pink ice skate with the icing. I add some green frosting polka dots and sprinkles before drowning my pancake in pure maple syrup. This reminds me of making Christmas cookies, except now I get to eat my pancakes right away… and with syrup!

Mom and Dad are busy creating their own works of art and laughing with one another. This seems like the perfect time to bring up taking a vacation.

"Mom, Dad?" I begin calmly. "This spring break Dacia is going to Vietnam and Becky is going to Florida. Do you think we can go anywhere?"

Mom and Dad look at one another with hesitation.

"I've got this one," Mom tells Dad.

"Khalli, honey, we would love to take a vacation with you. But we can't right now."

I take a deep breath and try to hide my frustration. This isn't the response I've been hoping for, but I imagine Mom is going to explain more.

"In a week, you have something very important happening."

"My first ice show!" I say excitedly.

"Exactly. And then the week after that you have another big event happening as you compete for the first time ever. So with the ice show and competition, you don't actually have time for a vacation."

I guess I didn't think about that at all…

"But there's always summer vacation, right?" I say, full of sudden hope.

Again Mom and Dad look at each other. Dad swallows hard.

"I'll take this one," he tells Mom.

"Khalli, do you remember a couple weeks ago when you had to take time off from skating? Do you remember the reason?"

"Because skating is really expensive and you had your overtime hours cut at work."

"Exactly. Your mom and I are working really hard to adjust our budget to give you the chance to have your dream. We don't ever want you to wish you would have had the chance to skate, we want to give you that chance. And for us, it's worth the sacrifices to see you so happy and to watch you grow in the sport. But one of the things we have to give up is the chance to travel and take vacations or even weekend getaways. For us it's one-hundred-percent worth it. I guess the real question becomes, is it worth it to you? Is the chance to skate and to take the lessons you want worth not going on vacation? Is it worth giving up some nice but expensive things for your dream? Because if you decide it is, then Mom and I will do everything we can to help you get the skating time and lessons you need. But if it's not, if you would rather be a normal kid and take vacations and go on shopping sprees with your friends, it's not too late to change your mind. But we ask that you understand that we are all in this together, so if skating is ever something you don't want anymore, we need you to let us know."

"Skating is everything that I want. I would love a vacation, but if I have to choose, I want to skate. I was bummed that Mom only had fifteen dollars for me at the mall yesterday, but if it meant having a skating lesson that morning, I want the skating lesson, not the shopping. I'm sorry I asked."

"Don't be sorry, honey," Mom steps in. "We are glad you love to skate, and we don't ever want to burden you with adult concerns, we just want you to understand. We wish we could give you everything, we really do. But we are doing our absolute best to give you your dream."

"I love you, guys!" I give both of my parents a hug. I guess I never really thought of all the sacrifices they are making so that I can skate. I wonder if I can find a way to make it up to them…

# CHAPTER 16

## *Just Call Me a Tornado!*

"Khalli… Khalli?"

"Aghhhhhhhhhh!"

"Khalli, honey. Do you want to skate today?"

"Is it morning already?" I shoot up straight in my bed, almost banging my head into Mom.

"Whoa! Calm down," Mom says with a gentle smile. "You still have time to get to the rink, you'll just need to move a little faster than usual. But today is only practice, so if you want to sleep instead, you won't miss a lesson."

"Only practice? But practice is so important if I'm going to improve. Coach Marie said I should practice several hours on my own for every lesson I have."

"I don't even know why I suggested taking today easy." Mom laughs.

"I don't know either…" I joke as dryly as possible.

"I'm ready when you are. I'll go warm up the car," Mom announces as she leaves my room.

I must have slept through my alarm. I need to practice so that I'm ready for my lesson with Coach Marie tomorrow.

She gave me homework, as always. I have a 3-turn pattern for my next skills test to improve as well as some spin combinations. And the Lutz, of course! This morning will be busy at the rink…

*****

At school, Mrs. Hill asks us to clear our desks.

"I know it's Monday, but I thought this would be a perfect day for a pop quiz."

"WHAT?" students gasp across the classroom.

Mrs. Hill smiles. "I'm only joking, well…part-joking. We are having a pop quiz, but it's not for a grade. As we enter our new science unit, I want to see what you already know."

Mrs. Hill passes out a quiz on weather and climate. There are questions about different types of clouds, the climate zones, and the water cycle. It's safe to say I don't know as much about weather as I thought I did. This quiz is difficult!

The quiz is only one sheet of paper, one-sided. Most of the answers are multiple choice, and I'm still struggling. Mrs. Hill gives us ten whole minutes to complete it.

"If you finish early, please just turn your paper over and draw a picture of weather."

Draw a picture of weather? What does that even mean? Like, draw raindrops or sunshine? Basically just draw an outdoor picture, I assume… Hmmmm. What to draw…

I know. I'll draw a tornado. They remind me of spins in figure skating—travelled spins that aren't very good, but spins nonetheless.

When you spin in skating, you are skating on a very tight backwards edge, so your blade makes little circles on the ice. The goal is to have the circles trace one on top of the other. It doesn't, however, always work out that way. Sometimes, if you get too high on your toe pick or if you don't press consistently or in the right spot of your blade, your spin travels. Travelling just means that your spin doesn't stay in the same spot.

I draw my tornado. After finishing, I add a figure skater at the bottom of the tornado. I can't help but smile at my picture.

Mrs. Hill comes around to collect our quizzes and flips them over to peek at our pictures in the process.

"Hmmmmmm," I hear as she inspects my artwork.

"It's a tornado…and a spin," I say proudly.

"Which direction do you rotate when you spin?" Mrs. Hill asks me.

"I rotate counterclockwise. Most skaters do, but some prefer the other direction. It's really up to each individual skater."

"Then you're basically a tornado."

"I don't get it. Can you please explain?" I ask politely.

Mrs. Hill grins. "We'll talk more about patterns in this unit, but since you're asking now…most tornadoes in the northern hemisphere rotate counterclockwise. In tornadoes, we call that direction cyclonically. Actually, about 95 percent of tornadoes rotate the same direction as you spin on the ice."

"Really?" Wow, I spin like a tornado! This weather unit could end up being really interesting after all!

# CHAPTER 17

## *Surprises*

Coach Marie rescheduled my Tuesday morning lesson to Wednesday afternoon. I'm super bummed because I am always looking forward to lessons with Coach Marie. I don't like that I have to wait an extra day and a half.

"She told me she wants to make sure you don't have to rush off to school right after you get off the ice," my mom tells me.

I feel like Mom knows something she's not telling me, but I have no idea what.

On Wednesday, we head straight to the rink after school. My lesson starts at 3:30, but if I hurry, I can have a little bit of time to warm up before I start with my coach.

I only have about ten minutes, and suddenly Coach Marie is there and ready.

"Thanks for moving your lesson, although I missed working with you yesterday morning," she tells me.

"Did you have to schedule someone else yesterday morning?"

"Actually, I wanted you during this time. I'll explain later. Right now let's focus on those 3-turns that you were supposed to work on and then your program. The dress rehearsal for the show is only two days away, and then come Saturday, you'll be rocking your program for the world for the first time!"

"For the world?" I ask nervously.

"I just meant that you'll be performing it for the first time ever. Sorry! I didn't mean to make you nervous." Coach Marie smiles gently.

We work through our entire lesson and my program. Coach Marie is very happy with my progress.

"All right, Khalli, I have another lesson. I want you to skate until the end of this session, and then at 4:45, I want you to get your skates off as quickly as possible and meet me in the lobby."

"Okay. Why?" I ask curiously.

Coach Marie gives me a mischievous grin. "You'll see. Now focus hard on what we've talked about today as you practice."

I'm doing my absolute best to focus. But why does she need to meet me off ice? Am I in trouble? Mom knows about whatever it is. Is it a parent-meeting? What could I have done wrong? Am I not progressing quickly enough?

Hundreds of questions fill my head, and I realize I'm not focusing on my skating at all.

*Focus!* I tell myself. *Whatever it is, you'll know soon enough, and if you were really in trouble, Coach Marie probably wouldn't have been smiling when she told you to hurry after practice.*

After practice, I rush to take my skates off and hurry to the lobby to meet my coach.

Coach Marie is already standing there ready to go. How is she so fast?

"Are you ready, Khalli?"

"I don't know what I'm ready for, but yes!" I smile boldly.

"I love how eager you are! All right...we are starting off-ice Axels today."

"Really? You're serious!" I can hardly contain myself. I realize I'm jumping up and down.

"That energy level is going to get you far!" Coach Marie tells me definitively.

Coach Marie starts me off with some basic hopping exercises and then progresses into harder and harder skills. An Axel is one and a half rotations. The jump takes off forward and then lands backward after turning one and a half times. Coach Marie wants me to kick my right leg forward but then transfer my weight over that same leg. It sounds so confusing, but as she walks me through the jump, it becomes clearer and clearer.

After a bunch of different exercises, she tells me I'm ready to give it a try. I start off just like I would do a waltz jump—the most basic half-rotation skating jump that there is. Then I climb into the air with my right leg. I pull my body over my right leg so that my left hip is slightly higher, and then I pull my body straight and tight. I come down and hit the ground facing sideways.

"Not bad, Khalli! You are only a quarter-rotation short! I want you to try a few more. I don't expect you to get this right away, but I want to give you a solid-enough base so that you can work on these at home. I know, once you get started, there's no stopping you, so I want to make sure you're practicing correctly."

Coach Marie watches me do about a dozen more. I complete two Axels that she says are fully rotated.

"I'm quite impressed, Khalli. This is great for day one. Once you are consistently landing these off ice, we'll put them on the ice. But until then, I want you to focus on your other skills on ice. I promise to let you know when you're ready. Okay?"

I nod excitedly. I cannot believe that I am actually working on my Axel already! Landing the Axel is a huge benchmark in the skating world. I can't wait until I can successfully do it on ice!

# CHAPTER 18

## *Dress Rehearsal*

The school days on Thursday and Friday seem to drag. I have been waiting forever for my first ice show; focusing in school is so difficult when you're this excited!

After school on Friday, Mom picks Becky and me up.

"I know you always walk home together, but I thought I'd give you a ride so you can get home quicker and start your homework, Khalli. You'll be at the rink all weekend, so unless you want to bring your homework along, you really need to finish it this afternoon before your dress rehearsal."

"We didn't get homework this weekend!" Becky announces.

Mom glances at both of us with a raised eyebrow. "None at all?"

"Nope. Today was that last day of third quarter, so Mrs. Hill said she wouldn't give homework again until next week… although she has lots of homework as the teacher, I'll bet."

"I imagine you're right," Mom agrees. "I guess I didn't need to pick you two up," Mom winks.

"Can you just drop me off at Becky's house? Since I'll be at the rink all weekend, I'll miss my best friend time."

"I would love that!" Becky exclaims. "But you can only stay for an hour, then my mom is taking me to Dacia's house. Do you want me to call her mom and see if you can join?"

I look at my mom, hoping for a yes.

"Sorry, honey, you have to be at the rink at 5:30 tonight, so it'd only be for a very short time, and Dacia lives on the other side of town from the rink. I'd like some time at home since I'll be gone at the rink all weekend too."

I raise my head to argue and then remember the talk my family just had about sacrifices on Sunday. Mom is already giving up so much so that I can skate and have my dream—I should be showing my appreciation.

"I understand," I say as positively as possible.

Becky looks at me confused. "My friends are all growing up and getting so old and mature," she announces in her best little old lady voice.

I giggle but deep inside wonder if she thinks about her family and their commitments the same way I now think about mine.

*****

"Let's go! Everyone in locker room 3! Hurry, ladies and gents! We've got a lot to do! Locker room 3! Let's go!" A group of coaches are shouting orders over the excitement of the kids as they try to round up all of the skaters.

"Take a seat, quiet please!" Coach Marie calls as soon as all of us are in locker room 3.

"We have a lot to do today, everyone! So I need you to quiet down and focus." Coach Marie pauses, waiting for everyone to stop talking. "I need you all to listen very closely for directions. I will not repeat myself." She glances around to make sure everyone understands and is listening to her.

"You have all been assigned a locker room already. Group-lesson girls are in locker rooms 1 and 2. Advanced girls are in locker room 3. All boys are in locker room 4. Female skaters over eighteen in room 5. If you are not on the ice, you are to stay in your locker room or to sit at the designated area for watching. I should not see anyone running around the rink at any point in time. If you are in your locker room or watching with the group, we will always be able to find you—and we need to always know where to find you. Do we all understand?"

Coach Marie watches strictly as we all nod our heads. Then she points to a small poster at the locker room door.

"Every locker room has a poster like this. This is the show order. Please make sure you know when you are performing and watch the order as we move through the show. You are expected to have your skates on at least twenty minutes before you are set to perform. You also need to have your dress or costume and skates on for the finale—we will learn the finale first tonight, and then we will do a full run-through of the show."

We are going to learn the entire finale tonight? What if I can't learn it that quickly? I wonder if I should raise my hand and ask.

I look around; no one else seems worried. If the really little kids in group lessons can learn it, then I should be able to learn it… I hope.

Coach Marie explains the job of the locker room monitors and the coaches and tells us whom we should see for questions.

"All right, who can tell me what we are doing first tonight?"

About half of the hands shoot up in the room.

"Only half of you know?" Coach Marie looks concerned.

Slowly, the rest of the hands go up.

"That looks more reassuring," my coach smiles. "Jenna, please tell everyone what's first."

"The finale," a young girl from group lessons announces confidently.

"Very good. Thank you, Jenna."

I see Jenna smiling proudly and realize I know that feeling. Praise from Coach Marie always feels great, especially since she's so strict.

"All right, I need everyone to meet me on the ice after these directions." Coach Marie pauses to make sure everyone is still listening.

"Skaters in group lessons, you will go to the ice and line up on the two blue hockey lines that stretch across the ice.

Advanced skaters, you will line up on the center circle. Are there any questions?"

Once she is sure there aren't any questions, Coach Marie sends us to the ice, and we take our spot just as she said.

The finale ends up being very easy to learn. I guess the coaches thought about how quickly we had to learn it when they choreographed it. It was way easier than my program!

We are skating to an old pop song. I recognize it from Auntie's Liz's radio station but am not sure what it's called. It's super upbeat and fun to skate to. I think it's a 2000s boy band. I'm sure Auntie Liz knows every word…

For the finale, the beginner skaters (how cool that I'm not considered a beginner anymore!) do mostly forward skating and follow each other making a train. They have some basic spins and half jumps, but it's kept quite simple. The advanced skaters (*me!*) show off their jumps and spins, but somehow the coaches designed it so we are never in each other's way. At the very end, we form a straight line and bow in groups so that each level is recognized. I think it's a perfect way to end the show!

"Nice work, skaters! All right, now that we have the finale down, we are going to start from the top! We will run the entire show through the finale just like we will tomorrow."

Coach Marie explains some final details, and we start from the top. I can't believe tomorrow is the show already!

# CHAPTER 19

## *Skate Like No One Is Watching*

Last night's dress rehearsal went really late. I drag myself out of bed after sleeping in on Saturday morning. Mom and Dad suggested I skip morning practice since today was already going to be a long day. I didn't agree with them, until they suggested I would skate with more energy if I wasn't so tired. They are probably right, and I really am so tired. A Saturday morning in my bed is most likely exactly what I need.

For the show rehearsal last night, they turned the rink lights out, and we skated in spotlights—it was like something straight out of my dreams! Skating under the spotlights was so weird. Everything around me was dark, and it was like I was always heading into the darkness, jumping into nothingness, but then the light always seemed to catch up. It threw me off a little, but I still landed everything and skated well—thank goodness, or I would be super nervous for tonight!

Our show tonight is at 7:00 p.m. Berger Lake Ice Center has so much seating that we only need to do one show whereas a lot of rinks have multiple shows. I wonder how many people will actually come.

Becky and Dacia are coming tonight before leaving for their spring break vacations tomorrow, and I cannot wait to show them how hard I've been working! They've never seen me skate, at least not since I first started. I've improved so much!

I lay in bed until 9:00 a.m. It's been weeks since I've slept this late! Just as I'm wondering if I could possibly fall back to sleep, Mom pokes her head into my room.

"Khalli, honey, would you like breakfast?"

"I always want breakfast!" I say, launching my suddenly wide awake body out of bed.

As Mom opens my door further, the aroma of bacon overtakes me. I love bacon! I wonder what else Mom made for breakfast.

I hurry down the stairs to a kitchen table maxed out with bacon, eggs, waffles, and fruit salad. There's a glass of fresh squeezed orange juice waiting for me, tea for Mom, and coffee for Dad.

"We want to make sure our shining star eats like the celebrity she is this morning. I have no idea how celebrities actually eat, so you'll have to let me know if I missed anything!" Dad jokes.

I haven't even performed yet, and Dad is already treating me like a star! Wait until after I rock this ice show!

I dig in. I always have such an appetite in the morning, but after the rehearsal last night, I'm even hungrier than usual! Two waffles, a plate full of eggs and bacon, and an overflowing bowl of fruit salad—I feel ready to face the day!

I look up from my plate after I wipe my face and see Mom and Dad both staring at me.

"Want some more?" Dad laughs.

"I couldn't eat any more if I tried."

"That's too bad!"

Dad pulls a plate from behind his back with my favorite doughnut waiting for me. A vanilla long john!

"Well, maybe another few bites." I reach for the doughnut.

Good thing my show isn't until later tonight, because I am signing myself up for a stomachache before I even take a bite. Worth it!

*****

It's a good thing I ate so much this morning because as the day went on, I got more and more nervous, too nervous to eat. I didn't know what to do to distract myself.

It's 5:45 p.m. and my parents are about to drop me off at the rink.

"And you have your dress?"

I nod.

"And tights?" Mom is going through a checklist.

"I have everything I need, Mom. Except my calm. I can't stop shaking!" I tell my mom nervously.

Mom seems confused.

"But this is just for fun, Khalli. It doesn't matter as much as your test, and you kept your nerves together then."

"I know. But no one was watching then. Now my friends are coming, their parents, my grandparents, and who knows who else. I wish I wouldn't have told everyone about this!"

Mom smiles boldly. "You're going to be great! I can't wait to show off my daughter!"

I smile back. I don't have the heart to tell her that's exactly why I'm nervous. Mom has made such a big deal about this with our family and friends. At first I thought that was great, but now that so many people are coming, I'm afraid I may not do well. What if I mess up and disappoint everyone? This is my first time performing my program. What if everything goes wrong?

I jump out of the car and grab my things from the trunk. I give my parents a forced, bold smile and fake my enthusiasm. "I'll see you after the show!"

"You're going to be great!" Mom and Dad cheer.

*I hope so*, I think to myself as I nervously saunter to locker room 3.

The locker room is nearly empty, no skaters, just a couple bags and dresses. I'm about ten minutes early, so I'm guessing everyone will rush in at the last minute. I sit down and try to focus on staying calm.

*Deep breaths*, I tell myself.

Inhale.

Exhale.

Slower. Calm. Breathe. Focus.

I talk myself down from the nerves, and my shaking slows.

"I'm *sooo* excited! Did you know Jessica is going to perform? I haven't seen her skate since she left for college. It's going to be epic! Oh…*hi, Khalli*!" Yana and Stacy burst through the door full of laughter and energy.

"Want to come warm up with us, Khalli?"

I nod coolly, trying to keep my nerves hidden. What is going on with my head today?

Together with Yana and Stacy, I jog down the locker room hallway. When we get to the end, Yana pulls her phone out and turns up the music. We do a full-body warm-up similar to the way Coach Marie warmed me up for my test last month. After we are warm, we take turns stretching each other's spiral positions, and then we each do a couple off-ice jumps.

"Your first ice show! Are you excited, Khalli?" Yana asks with a glowing smile as Stacy jogs off to do her hair.

"I think so," I tell her nervously.

"You're really nervous, aren't you?"

"Completely," I admit shyly.

"Your program is so strong and consistent. I know you can do this."

"But my entire family and so many of my friends are watching. They've never seen me skate. My parents have been bragging about me so much, and now I don't want to let them down."

"But it's not about them," Yana tells me boldly.

"What?"

"It's about you. It's about your chance to show the audience that you love this sport and that you're good at it. And you are. But if you get nervous, then just skate like no one is watching! Perform well for yourself, not for them. Once you get good at that, you can start performing for everyone else too."

I nod nervously. What Yana is telling me makes sense, but I'm too overwhelmed right now to absorb her advice.

"Twenty minutes! The show starts in twenty minutes!" Coach Marie calls through the locker room hallway.

Wow! Where did the time go? I don't know if I'm ready.

"Come on, let's go do our makeup together!" Yana grabs my hand and pulls me to the locker room. "If you stay busy, maybe you won't feel as nervous."

I certainly hope so.

# CHAPTER 20

## *Showtime!*

Coach Jessica pokes her head into the restroom as Yana and I are doing our makeup in front of the mirror. Yana has dumped her entire makeup bag into the sink for easy access to everything; she has so much stuff! I'm basically just doing lipstick and mascara because that's all I know how to do well.

"You ladies look beautiful! How are you feeling?"

"I'm so excited to watch you skate!" Yana bursts out.

Coach Jessica smiles and thanks her. "And you, Khalli, this is your first big performance! I'm so excited for you, you're going to have so much fun!"

I smile nervously back.

"It's totally okay to be nervous, Khalli," Jessica reassures me. "Just don't let your nerves control you or take the enjoyment out of today. Have fun!"

"I'll try," I promise, but I secretly question if Coach Jessica really even knows what fun actually is—because this definitely isn't it! My stomach is in knots. I feel like I could actually throw up any minute.

"Five minutes!" Coach Marie yells through the doorway.

She's so busy running the show that I don't anticipate she'll have any time to help me the way she normally does. Thank goodness Yana is here with me. I don't know if I'd manage to make it through these nerves if it weren't for her.

Coach Jessica leaves to lace up her skates. I want to keep talking with her to stay calm, but she's clearly very focused. Since she's the guest performer, she'll be skating first. She said after she skates, she will help the younger skaters in group numbers make it out on the ice for their numbers. I really hope she has some time to help me as well.

Yana and I finish our makeup and head through the door into our locker room. Stacy and Tamerah burst in from the hallway.

"We're going to go watch Jessica. Are you coming?" Stacy practically squeals to Yana.

"Absolutely! C'mon, Khalli," Yana invites me to join.

We step out to the ice just in time to hear the National Anthem. Standing at the edge of the ice and looking across to the massive audience, I suddenly feel my entire body starting to shake. There are so many people!

As soon as the anthem is over, the announcer introduces the guest skater—my coach!

"And please put your hands together for lifelong Berger Lake Ice Center Club member and national triple gold medalist, Jessica James!"

"*Eeeeeeeeee!*" Stacy, Tamerah, and Yana are screaming and cheering her on right next to me.

I clap and try to get excited for her, but I'm just too nervous!

Her music starts, and oh my God, is she graceful! I've never seen Coach Jessica skate before; she is literally dancing across the ice, just floating through crazy complicated footwork. Triple Salchow! Wow! Camel, Biellmann, back sit! Perfection! I can't believe how incredible she is! Coach Marie and everyone else have said she is good, but—double Axel—triple toe! Amazing!

When she finishes, I jump to my feet, screaming in awe! Wow, just wow! I want to skate like that!

"Time to hurry," Yana whispers as soon as the cheering calms down. "You're on after just a few skaters."

And the nerves are back. I completely forgot how nauseous I felt after my coach started skating, but now I think I'm going to throw up. And pee. Man, do I have to pee!

"Do you think I have enough time to go to the bathroom?" I ask Yana.

"Yeah, but you really don't have to go. It's just nerves."

"No. Trust me. I have to go!" I sprint off into the locker room.

When I walk out the locker room door a minute later, Coach Marie is in the hallway waiting for me.

"Khalli! I'm so excited for your first performance. Are you excited?"

"Nervous," I manage to squeak.

"Nerves are good. Remember, that means you care. What I'm excited about is getting to see your determination shine in front of an audience. This is where you get to prove to yourself that you can be as focused as I know you can be. You're going to be great. C'mon, let's do this together. I'll be cheering for you the entire time!" And with that, Coach Marie opens the door to the ice. "It's showtime!" She smiles.

"Taking the ice, please welcome one of our newest skaters at Berger Lake Ice Center, Khalli Davies!"

That's my cue. It's time.

I stroke rigidly to my starting position in the center of the ice. It feels like my knees are locked; everything is so stiff. I strike my starting pose and look out into the crowd. I can't seem to find my family or friends. I squint to see into the darkness beyond the spotlight, and suddenly my music begins.

I push off. My first jump is my Salchow—easy. Connecting footwork into a scratch spin, a little travelled, but I've got this. Pressure through the skating foot, belly button to my spine, tension through the arms as I pull in—change to a back spin. Decent. Next my spirals, which will connect me into my hardest combo, the loop-loop.

My backward outside spiral glides along the boards right in front of the audience. This is my chance to search the crowd for my family and friends. Becky and Dacia are right in front of me!

"Go Khalli!"

They are holding a sign; I don't have a chance to read it as I zip by, but their screams are enough for encouragement. Okay, loop-loop. I set up, bend into my ankles, and up! My first jump is easy as can be. I begin to rebend for the second, and suddenly everything goes dark around me!

*Commit!* I beg of myself.

I leave the ice and…*flash*! The spotlight finds me again in midair. When the light hits me, my natural reaction is panic—I flail, unintentionally opening my air position. As soon as I start to bail, I realize my mistake, but it's too late. I come out of the second loop facing forward—nose-diving at the ice! I try to save it, hook my toe pick in the process, and end up bashing into the ice on my right hip. Better than my face. I'm surrounded by darkness until…there it is. The spotlight finds me…on my butt…in front of five hundred people. I scramble to get up.

I need to finish this program.

The entire audience cheers as I scramble to my feet. Are they applauding my fall?

Pushing aggressively down the ice, I make it to my footwork just on time. The footwork is difficult, and I'm frazzled. It's time to focus. My choreography takes me right in front of Coach Marie. The scratchy panic of my blades can be heard by all; skating should never sound scratchy, especially not *this* scratchy!

"You can do this, Khalli. Focus!" she shouts sternly as I whiz past.

*I know*, I respond silently in my head, more for my sake than for my coach.

Toe loop—falling leaf—toe loop. Fighting to make my split position in the falling leaf as big as possible, I point my toes as hard as possible through the air. I have my pride to regain!

I plow through the rest of my program full energy, striving to get my head fully in the game. My final element is a sit spin. I snap my right leg around, dropping as low as I can. Nearly sitting on my ankle, I fight to hold my position. There's so much music left! When the nerves kicked in, I must have begun rushing too fast through my program. Now I have to hold my spin forever in order to end with the music! I fight to hold my spin; I'm running out of speed! Should I come up? Should I stay in the sit position? This has never happened before!

I decide to stay.

There are about eight seconds left. I can rise into a scratch spin now and finish with the music.

And up! C'mon! Why can't I get up? I don't have enough strength or speed left to push myself up. What now?

I set my second foot down, put my hands on my knees, and push up using my entire body. I know this looks ugly, but I am not going to sit down on the ice…not again! I'm finally fully upright just as the music ends.

That was the worst I have ever skated my program!

"*Yessssss!* Woo! Way to go, Khalli!" Blares towards me from the audience.

But I wasn't good; I wasn't good at all.

I try to fake a smile for the crowd as I hold my ending pose. But I can't. I whip around to exit the ice, just as the first tear rolls down my cheek.

I've failed. The one time I get to show my friends and family why I've been at the rink so much, and I blow it. I literally couldn't have skated any worse.

# CHAPTER 21

## *It's Only Up from Here*

"You were so good!" Becky raves, running up to me after the show. "I didn't know you could do all that in skates!"

Trying to smile, I give her a hug. "Thanks, but I'm not happy with how I skated. I'm so much better than that, I swear."

"Is it because you fell?" Dacia asks. "I didn't see you go down, but then suddenly the spotlight was shining on you when you were on your butt. Wait… I didn't mean it like that, like it spotlighted you on your butt. I meant the light caught up to you…after you fell. I mean, not that I'm highlighting your fall, I—"

"Dacia—stop talking!" Becky interjects.

I try to smile. "It's okay, Becky. Dacia's right. I fell. Everyone saw. It was horrible."

"But everything else was so good. I had no idea how much you could do—and if that was a bad skate, I can only imagine how good you actually are," Becky is trying so hard to make me feel better.

"And we got you flowers," Dacia passes me a bouquet of colorful carnations.

"Thanks, but I didn't really earn flowers."

"Yes, you did. Now take them, stop talking, and smile for a picture with us!" Becky insists.

I fake my best smile for their sake. I don't think they understand how truly disappointed I am with myself.

*****

I dragged myself through the weekend. Both Becky and Dacia left for their vacations on Sunday, and there was nothing Mom or Dad could do to get me out of this slump—a slump I created all by myself, because that's what I do best. I fail.

Monday morning starts extra early. Another lesson with Coach Marie. We didn't really get to talk much after the show, but I imagine she's disappointed in me. My skating reflects on her. I've never dreaded a lesson so much before.

I lace up my skates slowly. I'm in no rush today.

"Good morning, Khalli!" Coach Marie calls cheerfully as I skate over to her.

I hang my head and mutter, "Good morning," back.

"Hey! Head up! This is not the Khalli I know."

"I'm so sorry I made you look bad at the ice show. How mad are you?" I finally muster up the words to say.

"Mad? Why would you think I'm mad?" my coach asks with confusion.

"I fell, I made you look bad. You prepared me to be better than how I skated."

"I'm not mad."

"But you're disappointed in me."

"No, Khalli. I'm not disappointed in you. I'm disappointed for you—I know how badly you wanted to skate better than how you did. I know how hard you've worked and how important this was to you. I also know you gave it your all, but your nerves won. And after they started to win, they took over."

"I didn't even feel like myself skating. It was horrible."

"It wasn't horrible. Although it wasn't exactly the performance of the year," Coach Marie scrunches her face jokingly throughout her second sentence, trying to lighten the mood. It doesn't work.

"Hey." She puts her hand on my shoulder and looks me square in the eyes. "You'll get there—I guarantee it. Someday, you'll be able to skate cleanly, even in front of a full house. But you have to start somewhere, and many of us, just like you, have a rough start. But you can only go up from here—and you will. I promise."

Her face is as genuine as it can be as she promises me she'll help me do better. She's made such a difference in my skating so far. I suppose I have no reason not to believe her.

"Okay," I state, rather solemnly. "But I'd like to get there by next weekend. I'd like to skate well for the competition."

Coach Marie nods. "Let's get to work then and see what we can make happen this week. Starting now, your time to sulk is officially over. It's go time!"

# CHAPTER 22

## *Determination*

Coach Marie was not going to let me revel in my failure and disappointment. She helped me create a plan to put my best foot forward at Saturday's competition. And with my school being on spring break, I have considerably more time to practice than usual. I've decided if Coach Marie believes in me, then I believe in me. I will redeem myself from my ice show performance by rocking it at the competition!

I have four hours of ice each day this week. Mom felt that was going to be too much, but I promised her both my mind and body could handle it. Friday, I am scheduling only one hour, to give my body time to rest before I compete. I know Mom wanted to schedule less ice for me, but after last weekend, I honestly think she's just happy to see me excited about skating again. So she bought me all the ice time I requested.

Coach Marie has been working me up to double run-throughs for the last month by adding more and more laps after I complete my program. We've done a couple programs back-to-back, leaving out the jumps and the spins in the second run-through. Today it's time for my first official full double run-through. This means doing my entire program twice, back-to-back, all elements included.

I put so much energy into doing the first run-through of my program the best I can, and as a result, I'm completely winded after doing it once. How will I manage a second time? But it's time to find out!

Thirty seconds into my second program, my legs start to feel like Jell-O.

"Breathe, Khalli!" Coach Marie is shouting at me.

I have this thing where when I focus too hard, I forget to breathe—kind of an issue when you're an athlete. We even worked out some areas in my program where my primary job is to calm my breathing. The spirals are one of those spots, and I just missed it!

I try to take a deep breath, but it's so hard. I'm winded, and therefore my breaths seem shallow and ineffective. It's like I can't get air into my lungs.

My footwork seems next to impossible right now! I feel like I'm trying to fling one limp spaghetti noodle leg over the other soggy noodle leg. How on earth does Tamerah skate double run-throughs of her four-minute program? Her jumps and spins are so much harder and require way more energy than mine too!

My sit spin is as wonky as can be at the end—but I made it!

I hold my ending pose as Coach Marie has taught me and then nearly collapse on the way back to my water bottle.

"One lap! Go!" my coach is yelling.

You've got to be kidding me!

I want nothing more than to collapse against the boards, but I know Coach Marie wants me to improve as badly as I want to improve. I need to do as she asks.

Taking a quick gasp for air, I push off into my lap. It literally takes every ounce of energy I have to make it around the rink. But I do, once again proving to myself that I always have more in me than I might believe.

"Grab a drink, we'll talk as you catch your breath." Coach Marie picks apart my program, gives me some homework, but overall says she's pleased with my first double run-through. Since I still have another two hours of ice today, she asks that I try one more double run-through.

"Not right now, but before you leave for the day," she requires of me.

I nod. I want to be as ready as possible for Saturday. There's no way I want to look back at the week and wonder if I could have trained harder.

# CHAPTER 23

## *Full-Time Figure Skater, Part-Time Bored*

It's Thursday, and I've been pushing myself all week long! Four hours on ice, plus more time doing off ice at home. Lots of stretching of my aching, tired muscles because as they get stronger, they get tighter—unless I do my job to stretch. And you best believe I'm doing my job! My spirals have gotten higher just over the course of this week. My program has gotten more consistent. Double run-throughs don't fully kill me anymore, and the second run-through is usually clean!

I'm struggling to believe it's already Thursday afternoon and my spring break is almost over. I haven't even had a day to sleep in yet. Every day has been spent mostly at the ice rink, pushing my exhausted body to its limits. As tired as I am, I can't imagine any other way I would have rather spent my break!

I wonder how Becky is enjoying Florida with her grandparents. And what about Dacia in Vietnam—is she getting along with her cousins that she's just met? I haven't messaged them because I've been so busy, and I also didn't want to interrupt their family time—but I was hoping they would reach out to me. I wonder if they even miss me. Are they having so much fun they forgot about me?

I decide to shoot Becky a message.

*"Hey, Becky! How's Florida? I miss you! How is everything at your grandma and grandpa's house? Have you gone to the beach yet? I bet you're super tan!"*

I sit down to stretch, setting my phone down next to me so I can see when she replies. Lately I've been really pushing myself to be able to do the splits. It's taken a ton of effort, but I'm almost there.

Ten minutes into stretching and still no reply—weird. Normally I hear back within minutes.

I shove my phone in the pocket of my oversized hoodie and jog downstairs to make a snack while I wait for Becky's reply. Skating four hours a day makes me so hungry!

Mom is sitting at the kitchen table on her computer. Her red plastic reading glasses are perched halfway down her nose, blonde hair tucked behind her ears. She doesn't even look up.

Okay—I guess everyone can just ignore me today.

Reaching into the pantry, I grab the jar of peanut butter and the bread. I irritably smear the peanut butter sloppily onto both pieces of bread, ripping the bread in the process. Next I slice a banana to fill the sandwich. Just as I'm about to bite into it, I glance at Mom. She still hasn't moved.

In an effort to strike up a conversation and avoid boredom, I cut my sandwich in half, deciding to share with Mom.

I sit down next to her and slide her plate gently into place directly under her nose.

"No thanks, honey."

Okay… I guess I'll just eat it myself. I leave her half sitting in front of her as I chew my half of the sandwich as loudly as possible—the sticky peanut butter smacks off the roof of my mouth with ease.

Mom tilts her head and stares at me.

Success!

"You want to play a game, Mom? I was thinking Uno, but I'm really up for whatever right now. You can pick!" I say with as much enthusiasm as possible.

"As you can see, I'm kind of busy right now, Khalli."

"I can wait," I slur with a mouthful of food. "I've got all day."

"Khalli."

Wow! Mom's voice is laced with irritation as she returns her attention to the computer!

I wait calmly, despite the anxiousness running through my veins. Mom continues to ignore me.

*Smack!* This peanut butter has skill!

No response from Mom.

"Should I go pick out a game?"

Nothing.

"What are you working on, Mom? Maybe I can help—probably not, but maybe." I pause. Still no response. "I'm so bored." *Smack!*

The frustration is creeping into Mom's face. How much longer do I have to keep this up?

"Mom."

Nothing.

"Mom!"

Wow, that lady has some focus!

The plus side of Mom not wanting half the sandwich is more peanut butter for me to aggressively chew. Reaching across the table, I seize Mom's half of the sandwich, raise it to my mouth for a bite, and…*smack!*

Mom lurches over the table and snaps the sandwich from my grip. "You are so irritating! Listen!" *Smack!* Mom takes a bite of my peanut butter banana sandwich and smacks it between the roof of her mouth and her tongue over and over. "You are making me crazy, Khalli!"

"So can we play a game?" I ask, full of amusement. Mom usually doesn't get this frustrated. "It's Thursday of my spring break, and we haven't done anything fun together yet."

Mom looks confused. "Khalli, we went to the rink… today, yesterday, the day before yesterday, the day before that. We're going again tomorrow. That's fun."

"It's so much fun. But we don't do it together. We ride in the car together, but that's it. I want to hang out with my mom—is that so bad?"

Mom softens. "Okay, go grab a game or puzzle or something. Give me ten more minutes to finish this, and I'm all yours."

Success! I knew this would work.

"And here." Mom hands me the sandwich. "Eat this on your way to get whatever it is you're getting. But eat it in front of me again, and I'll '*smack*' you with it!" She playfully flicks an imaginary sandwich in my direction.

Point made.

Ten minutes later I come back with a puzzle to work on with Mom. She closes her laptop and scooches next to me to work.

Mom always starts with the border first. I decide to pick out pieces of the castle and focus on that. I have about twenty castle pieces set aside, and my phone starts to ring.

"It's Becky, I have to take this!"

Mom snatches my phone out of my hand and answers.

"Hi, Becky! It's Auntie Krista."

Becky's talking on the other end.

"Actually, no. Khalli just spent endless amounts of time irritating me in an effort to get me to do something with her, and now that I've set everything aside to entertain her, I'm holding her hostage from phone calls."

*What?*

I hear Becky's voice chattering softly.

"You should ask her about her sandwich-eating skills. That kid can smack her peanut butter like no one's business. And then she stole my sandwich. Who cares if she made it for me and I didn't want it? What nerve!"

I can hear Becky cracking up on the other line as Mom continues to rip on me and tell what I just did.

"I'll have her call you when we finish this puzzle, but until then, her phone is mine, as is her time! Have fun in

Florida, Becky! Please tell Liz hi for me!" And with that, Mom ends the call.

"Mom!" I practically screech.

"Fair is fair. Now I'm so glad we have some quality time together that is cutting into both of our plans." Mom grins, half laughing, half serious.

I guess we're doing a puzzle today. I shake my head in both disbelief and amusement at my sassy mother.

# CHAPTER 24

## *The Final Run-Through*

I only have one hour of practice ice today, and my exhausted body is rather grateful for the limited ice time. The rink is pretty quiet, by far the calmest it's been all week. Yana and Tamerah, the only other skaters who have been here all day, every day during spring break, have already come and gone.

Coach Marie will be working with me for thirty minutes today—my final lesson before tomorrow's competition. I can't believe I will compete already tomorrow! She's asked that I am fully warmed up before we begin, so I've scheduled my ice time with fifteen minutes before my lesson, and then fifteen minutes after to make any corrections she may give me.

"I want to start with your program, everything from how you get onto the ice and present yourself to the judges, all the way through your program until you exit the ice. Are you ready to go, like I've asked?"

Coach Marie is not messing around today. I nod confidently.

We've gone through this several times. The primary door to the ice for Brierton Arena, where I'm competing tomorrow (*ahhhh!)* is behind the goalie box area at the end of the rink. I will enter and exit through this door. The judges will be seated in the hockey box closest to the door. When I enter, I will first present to them, and then I'll present myself to the audience on the way to the red dot where I'll start my program. To present, I stretch my free leg as long as possible behind me, turning towards judges, and then the audience, with beautiful, elongated arms. Coach Marie has asked me to try to make eye contact. How scary is that! Then I pause in my starting position and wait for my music to start.

After completing my program, I am to hold my ending pose and count to five, smiling the entire time. After that, Coach Marie has given me the option to curtsy. For my first competition, I've chosen not to; I'm afraid I won't remember after putting such intense focus on my program! Then as I skate back to my coach. I present myself one more time and stroke off as nicely as possible, controlling my urge to race off.

My entire run-though goes smoothly, with the exception to one little stumble coming out of my front scratch back scratch spin.

Coach Marie is pleased. "Let's run that transition from the first spin through your loop-loop three more times. I just want to make sure you feel comfortable. I'll play the music."

Moana's voice blares over the sound system as I push into my scratch spin. Clean, easy, centered.

"Good, Khalli! Again!"

I do it well two more times.

"Well, I have no reason to believe you won't skate it just like that for the competition tomorrow. I feel confident you are completely prepared. How do you feel?"

"Way better than I did last weekend at the ice show," I reply. "The program feels so much easier—I think the double run-throughs have made me a lot stronger."

"Oh, I one-hundred-percent agree! I know they aren't fun, but they are worth it!"

"I just wish we could have been doing them going into the ice show."

My coach nods. "But you weren't physically ready yet. We've been working you up to this. You are ready now. You are so ready now that after this competition, I'd like to change your program and have you compete a level higher for the next competition."

"What?"

"That means, flip jumps, Lutz jumps, and more difficult spins. We'll see how you skate and place this time around, but I want you to work for a place on the podium, and in a couple months, you'll be leaving others at this level in the dust."

Suddenly I feel incredibly proud of my progress—I didn't realize I was improving this quickly! I want to skate well tomorrow so I can move up a level! I want my program to be more advanced, even if that means more work for me and tougher competition.

"What should I work on today during my fifteen minutes of practice?" I ask.

"If there's anything you want to do to feel more confident about your program, do that first. After that, work on the patterns from your next skills test. I know we didn't get to them today, but I've seen you pounding them this week and love the progress! I'd like to see if we can get you tested no later than midsummer."

Wow! Like my coach always says, "More practice, more progress!"

*****

Mom stayed and watched my practice and is raging with excitement after I get in the car.

"Khalli, your program looks so good! You're skating so much faster, and you are displaying artistry that I haven't seen yet from you."

"That's because I have an extra-picky coach!" I laugh. "Although she was quite happy with how I skated today."

"I'll bet! You skate like that tomorrow, and who knows what could happen!" Mom hints.

"I just want to skate my best. It's okay if I don't get a medal. After what happened at the ice show, I just want to feel proud of myself after the day is over."

Mom's face suddenly gets really soft.

"What's wrong, Mom?"

"Nothing's wrong… I was just thinking about how much you've changed this year, since you've started skating seriously anyway. I'm just so proud of how much you've matured. But you're not my little baby anymore." Mom wipes some moisture from under her eye. It isn't a full tear, but almost.

I grin. "Thanks, Mom."

My mom is definitely the emotions of the family. I feel proud, but I also hope she keeps herself together tomorrow and doesn't embarrass me with too many tears.

# CHAPTER 25

## *Raccoon-Ready*

Today's the day! My chance to prove I can do this and I can do it well! No more ice-show mishaps, no more mistakes. I am going to skate my best, just like I did every day in practice this week!

Brierton Arena is a little more than an hour away from our home. In addition to my skates, I've packed my dress, tights, makeup, and hair supplies, along with my headphones, so I can tune out everything around me and listen to my program music—the entire drive!

"Khalli, honey." Mom is twisted around from the front seat, tapping me above the knee softly.

I open my eyes, squinting immediately into the blazing sunlight.

"We're here, Khalli. Wake up."

It takes a minute for me to get my bearings as I look around me. A bunch of buildings I've never seen before. A big parking lot. Brierton Ice Arena. Oh! Duh! We're at the competition! I slept through the entire drive!

I jolt upright, reach for my bag on the seat, and scramble to get out of the car.

"Khalli, breathe!" Dad laughs from the driver's seat. "We have plenty of time. Remember, you wanted to be here an hour before Marie requested. You have time, a lot of time."

Oh, thank God!

Inside the arena, everything screams competition day! Skaters everywhere are scurrying about in colorful, sparkling dresses and costumes; some are proudly wearing medals around their necks—those are gorgeous medals! Some skaters are crying, others look nervous, and yet others look fiercely determined. That's the look I want! I adjust my face to look as determined as possible; no one needs to know this is my first competition and I'm the underdog! There are decorations on the walls and ceilings and vendors throughout the lobby selling dresses, event shirts, and other skating goods. There's a table with medals and trophies; behind it is the podium. A photographer works with skaters to pose them for individual shots as well as group shots. Looking to the right, I see the registration table. That's where I need to start.

"Mom!" I say pointing.

Mom and Dad follow me to the registration table, and we get checked in.

"Make sure you have your backup music rink side," I'm told as my name is checked off the list.

I look to Mom confused. "Don't worry, Khalli, I have it. Marie coached me through this the same way she coached you."

"I doubt it." I laugh. "Have you been doing double run-throughs?"

Mom's face looks repulsed. "Oh, absolutely not! You win. She's been harder on you, and she better continue to be harder on you!" Mom jokes back as we walk away.

"Khalli," the lady at the registration desk calls after us. "You forgot your goodie bag!" She reaches across the table to hand me a cute blue bag with the "Blades of Brierton Open" logo.

"Oh, we didn't order this," Mom says confidently.

"One bag is included for every competitor as our way of saying thank you for competing. Most competitions do this. Is this your first competition?" she asks me with a gentle smile.

Welp! There goes my I'm-confident-and-I-know-what-I'm-doing-here plan. Apparently, it's super obvious that this is my first competition!

"Yes," I reply quietly. I thank her, wondering silently what else I don't know about competing yet.

"Can we go look at the T-shirt booth?" I ask my parents, pointing. The booth is layered with different-colored shirts and sweatshirts.

"We definitely can later. But let's get your hair and makeup done first so that we don't have to rush later," Mom advises.

Seems like a decent plan, so I agree.

We find an empty table in the corner of the lobby, and Mom starts my makeup while Dad walks off to look around.

"Close your eyes," Mom orders.

I feel her smearing something across my eyelid ever so softly. It tickles. I can't help but giggle as the brush dances across my eyelid, pushing my lashes side to side.

"Stop moving!" Mom insists.

"I can't, it tickles. I swear, you're poking at my eyeball." I laugh, opening my one eye.

Mom is standing literally six inches from my nose, her face twisted sternly with both focus and irritation.

"Sorry, Mom, you can continue."

"Yes, Princess Khalli. At your service!" Mom mocks.

I feel wet goop run along the top of my lashes. My eye twitches uncontrollably. Fighting to hold still, I wait for my mom to pull her hand away from my face.

"Ew! What is that!?"

"Liquid eyeliner. Man, this sure is difficult to apply to someone else!"

"I'm really feeling confident about this," I reply with a hint of sarcasm.

"Hi Mrs. Davies! Hi Khalli! That looks…umm… okay…" I hear the hesitance in Yana's voice. "You should give her some eyeliner wings along her eyes!"

I squeak through my closed mouth in an attempt to acknowledge Yana. I'm too afraid that opening my mouth will mess Mom up, and by her shaking hand, it's clear she's struggling with the eyeliner.

Mom presses the brush against the side of my eye and draws a line out towards my temple.

"I'm not sure how to make that look right," Mom says discouraged as she adds more eyeliner around my eye to try to connect the line she just drew.

"Oww!" I screech as liquid starts running into my eye. "It burns!" My hand shoots up to my eye in reflex.

"Don't touch!" Mom shouts, clasping my hand in hers.

"Can I help?" Yana asks concerned. "I love doing makeup! I usually do Stacy's for competitions, and she keeps letting me do it, so that's proof enough that I'm not bad at it, right?"

Mom looks at me, clearly awaiting my approval.

"Can I see what Mom did first?"

"Absolutely!" Yana laughingly hands me a mirror.

I lift it to my face, and oh my God! My left eye looks like a raccoon! The pitch-black eyeliner extends halfway to the top of my ear. "That's a big wing, Mom!" I don't know whether to laugh or cry. If this weren't my big day, my chance to prove myself, this would be funny. But I look like a train wreck!

"Oh, goodness!" I hear Coach Marie as she approaches behind Mom.

"Don't worry, I'll fix it," Yana promises confidently.

"Please do," my coach insists as my mom turns beet red. "Yana, she's all yours. Krista, don't sweat it. Khalli will look great, and while Yana works on her, we'll go over the plan for today. And then I'll give you some tips for doing makeup on others. Maybe you two can practice at home with the eyeliner another day."

"Thank God for Coach Marie and damage control! And your mom will be fine," Yana says as she pulls me into the locker room to get a makeup wipe.

A group of girls laugh at me as we rush by.

"Don't worry about them, you're going to crush them on the ice!" Yana reassures me.

Twenty minutes later, Yana hands me the mirror to look at her final product. I find myself speechless as I take in the result of her efforts through my reflection. I have gorgeous ombré eyes, with deep purples, blues, and greens all blended perfectly together. The shimmering colors pull out the gold flecks in my brown eyes. My eyeliner has a small wing on the outside of each eye, tied perfectly into the ombré eye shadow. My brows are bold and cleanly lined. A rose-colored blush pulls out my cheekbones, and a deeper rose makes my lips pop. I don't know what to say—I've never looked this good in my life!

Yana is waiting patiently for my approval, but I'm too busy looking at myself to notice right away.

"Sooo…" she draws out the "o" until I finally react.

I look up with the biggest smile imaginable—and then look back to the mirror to see how I look smiling, which makes me smile even more.

"I think it's safe to say you like it," Yana boasts.

When I'm finally done admiring myself, I thank her repeatedly.

"How did you learn how to do this?" I ask full of curiosity.

"I watch a lot of makeup tutorials online. Coach Marie has always been so good at makeup, I guess I was inspired!" She laughs. "Now let's go show your mom!" She grabs my hand and pulls me back to the lobby, eager to show off her work of art.

Mom is so impressed and grateful with Yana's work. I think I'm hiring Yana for every competition and test from now on! Mom does my hair; this is definitely her skill set—makeup, apparently not so much. With ease, Mom braids a crown around my head and wraps it into a perfect bun.

"And the customer says…" Mom grins as she hands me a mirror to inspect her work.

I rotate the mirror as much as I can around my head. Perfection.

"I look fiercely ready!" I beam at my mom and dad.

# CHAPTER 26

## *Big Ugh!*

We walk around and window shop the booths, looking at all the merchandise. Everything is skating-related and beautiful, and… I want it all!

Mom and Dad give me time to look at everything and listen to all my excited thoughts on each product. When I find a small, inexpensive skating coin purse, I decide I need it. It's blue, purple, and green—very similar shades to the colors on my dress—and has a skater doing a Biellmann in diamond-like crystals. This would be perfect for keeping my extra cash at the rink; my mom always leaves a little with me in case I need to buy another ice session when she's not there or if I have an emergency and need something. The money often floats around my bag; this coin purse is perfect! I decide to ask my dad for it; he usually has a harder time telling me no than Mom.

Dad just smiles. "Not right now, Khalli. Let's just browse until your coach is ready for you. Don't you want to watch some of the other skaters?"

"I'm afraid watching will make me nervous. Can we stay in the lobby? I think I only have about ten minutes until

Coach Marie said she'd be ready for me. But after I compete, I would like to watch a few skaters—especially Yana. She skates two groups after me."

"Absolutely! It's your day, Khalli!"

We continue browsing the booths until Coach Marie comes and finds me admiring the dresses for sale.

"I like yours better!" my coach pipes from behind me, making me jump a bit. "How are you feeling, Khalli? Your hair and makeup look amazing—I love the braid!"

"Thanks! I'm a little nervous, but I feel incredibly prepared. I just need to do what I did in practice, right?"

"That's all you need to do," my coach confirms with a confident nod. "So let's get you ready! Have you looked at the ice yet?"

I shake my head.

"Okay, let's do that first."

I follow my coach into the arena and look around. There are so many people!

"This rink is the same size as what you've been practicing on. The only difference is, you'll enter on the other side—but that's how we practiced."

I look out at the rink. That is how we practiced, but I didn't expect the bleachers to be on the other side. I always come out of my first spin and skate towards the audience. But now the audience isn't there.

"Do I need to reverse my program after the spin?"

"Why would you do that?" Coach Marie asks delicately.

"So that I'm in the same spot on the ice, in front of the crowd."

"Don't think so hard about it, Khalli. Your program should feel, and be, exactly the same. Remember when we did your practice run-throughs for this competition and you got on the ice by the paint company advertisement, remember our fake door we made on the wall, and then you started your program facing the other direction, but everything was the same?"

I nod.

"Good, that's exactly what we're doing here. You'll start facing the audience, and then run your program exactly as you always have."

"So I *will* come out of my spin and go towards the audience?"

"You got it! Make sense?"

"Sure." I think it does. I really hope it does!

"All right. Let's get you ready then!"

Coach Marie wants me to put my dress on. "We'll wait to put your skates on for a bit, but let's get you fully ready otherwise. We can warm up once everything else is ready. I'll go check to make sure everything is still on time and check your skating order." And with that, my coach sends me away.

Coming out of the changing stall, I glance at the mirror as I walk past, halting myself in my tracks. Is that really me? Wow! I look so mature and professional! No one would guess by the look of me that this is my first competition!

"Look at my girl!" My dad picks me up and spins me when I enter the lobby.

"You look amazing!" Mom has a giddy smile plastered to her face.

"Future pair skater!" Coach Marie hints at our lift and then moves on with business. "You skate third out of nine skaters—that's a great place to be! You won't have time to get cold and stiff after your on-ice warm-up, and you'll have time to get your breath back after five aggressive minutes of warm-up. Let's warm you up and stretch off ice, and then we'll get your skates on." She turns to my parents, "We'll be back in ten minutes. I'll take her backup music from you when we return."

I follow her to a slightly quieter hallway behind the bleachers. "Keep your eyes open so you don't hit anyone when you're warming up your arms," my coach warns.

I follow my coach through a full-body warm-up, and she helps me stretch; then we head back to the lobby to find my parents. Coach Marie stops to check in with the ice monitor on the way, meeting me and my parents in the lobby a minute later.

"You're after this group. These skaters have three-minute programs, so you have almost twenty-five minutes before your on-ice warm-up. Let's get you ready for the ice! Run to the bathroom and lose the underwear, and then you can put your skates on."

I stare at my coach in utter confusion and, judging by her abrupt response, probably display some intense rejection through my facial expression.

"Your underwear are hanging out and showing through your tights. I don't want to see them. The judges and the audience don't want to see them. And I can guarantee, you won't want to see them when you watch the video later. You can cut them up higher or take them off—but no one wants to see them."

I look at my mom for help.

"I guess this pair won't work for skating dresses, something we didn't think about. Go take them off, Khalli. Your coach is right. I can see them, and I've never once seen them on a skater on TV. I don't have scissors, so I can't cut them."

I look at my mom beggingly.

"You have tights on, you'll be fine."

*Ugh! Big ugh!* I can't believe this! My first competition and I can't even wear my underwear! How embarrassing! So humiliating that I don't even want to ask other skaters if this has happened to them. *Ugh!*

When I come out of the bathroom, underwearless and uncomfortable, my coach nods.

"Now you look the part! You look ready, and you look like an experienced competitor. Now let's get ready to rock this! Skates on!"

# CHAPTER 27

## *In It to Win It*

Standing outside the edge of the rink, my coach directs me to mentally walk through my program while looking at the ice.

"Plan where you'll do each element, and then in your head, make yourself do the element, and do it well!"

What a mentally exhausting exercise!

"Five-minute warm-up!"

The ice monitor is calling each of my competitor's names and sending us out to the ice.

"Go ahead," my coach nods.

I have my warm-up fully planned out. First a lap to feel the ice—this ice feels a lot like the ice at Berger Lake; perfect! Then my spins followed by all my jumps with their intro choreography. Everything feels easy today; I do every element cleanly twice, and then it's time to move on.

"Start your program!" my coach encourages. "You have about two minutes left."

Nice! When we planned my warm-up out, we estimated only enough time to start my program. I have lots of time; the ice monitor hasn't even called one minute yet!

I start exactly where Coach Marie directed earlier, exactly how I walked through it in my mind just minutes ago. I finish my salchow and start skating towards my scratch spin, only to hear my name being called from the distance.

"Khalli! Stop!" Coach Marie is waving her arms at me.

I skate over to her.

My coach's voice softens, "That's not where your program goes, Khalli."

"I realize that now," I stammer in complete panic. "But everything feels backwards with the audience on the other side."

"They're not on the other side of you. You'll start facing them, just like you do at our rink."

"I know, but the door is on the other side."

"That it is. But the door doesn't matter, just the audience. Once you get to your starting position, nothing else changes."

"One minute, skaters!"

"Oh, that makes sense. I just need to turn around after I skate on."

My coach nods.

I skate back to my starting position and skate from the beginning through the loop-loop combo before being called off the ice.

"So much better!" my coach cheers with a sense of relief in her voice. She throws me a powerful high five. "Step back from the door, Khalli. Let's let the other two skaters before you through and give them some room."

Ahh! My competitors! I was so busy focusing during my warm-up that I didn't get a chance to look to see how many of the competitors were stronger skaters than me. One girl has a big water spot on her tights—I guess her warm-up included some falls. Maybe I have a chance to beat her!

"Let's take this time to focus on where your program will go one more time. I want you to ignore the skater performing right now and instead draw with your finger for me where your program will go. I want you to feel extra confident when you step on that ice in three minutes!"

I really wanted to watch my competitors, but I guess my coach has other plans. I do as she says, and she nods firmly.

"All right, Khalli, I'll take your jacket and gloves. You're after this skater. Any questions?"

"Do you think I can win?"

Coach Marie smiles. "I haven't seen all the other competitors yet, but I know you're performing your skills at a consistently high level, and your program is well choreographed, highlighting your skills." She winks as she praises her own choreography skills.

I think that means I have a shot! I hand my coach my gloves and jacket and take one final drink from my water bottle before stepping towards the rink door. I scan the crowd for my parents while I wait nervously. There they are! And they're with an entire group of Berger Lake families… I have a cheering section!

"Representing Berger Lake Ice Center, please welcome… Khalli Davies!"

That's me! It's go time. Coach Marie grabs my hand and looks me square in the eyes.

"I know you want this, Khalli, and you've worked so hard and prepared to the fullest extent possible. Now go get it!"

She lets go of my hand, and I stroke confidently to my starting position, taking a breath to present myself to the huge audience and the judges. There are even more people watching than at the ice show. This is my chance to redeem myself!

Standing in my starting pose, I inhale as deeply as possible and let it out as slowly as possible. And then the music begins.

My head is in thc game. I now understand the layout of the rink and where my program goes…at least I hope. I can do this. I focus and exaggerate my artistry through my entire program. Final spin…and done! Wow! That went fast! *One, two, three, four, five…* I count my ending pose as I listen to the immense cheering from the crowd. I did it! I really skated well! Turning to skate off, I really focus on my posture and form. Where's Coach Marie? Where's the door? I'm halfway to the edge of the rink but can't find the door—did they close it? I stop in my tracks, suddenly in a panic. How do I get off the ice?

"Go, Khalli! Yeah!" I hear from the audience.

I turn to the noise and suddenly see Yana swinging her arms to the other side of the rink, fingers pointed. I turn to see where she's pointing—the door! Of course, it's on the other side! I skate as confidently as possible back while the Berger Lake crowd continues cheering for me; my face is burning red from embarrassment. I hope Yana put this makeup on thick enough to hide my blushing!

One of my competitors snickers as I step off the ice. "Couldn't find the door, huh?" she laughs under her breath.

"Way to go, Khalli!" my coach gives me a huge hug. "I liked your victory lap at the end, but next time let's skip it, okay?"

"I got lost!" I blurt loudly, my voice jacked with adrenaline.

"I know. It's okay. You nailed your program! The judges weren't even watching you get off, they were too busy writing, so don't sweat it. Your program was beautiful!"

My parents run over to hug me. Yana is right behind them.

"Yana, you're with me now! Khalli, I'll be back with you to check scores once Yana is ready," my coach announces.

"Okay, I'll go change while I wait for results."

"No, you won't! With as well as you skated, you need to keep your skates on until results are up."

"Why?"

"I'll tell you later. Why don't you go and watch the rest of your group until then. And, Khalli"—she pauses to make sure I'm listening—"I'm so very proud of you!"

I can't stop smiling as I put my guards over my blades and head to the bleachers with my parents. Everyone from Berger Lake cheers me on and fills me with compliments when I arrive.

"So far you've been the best!" Yana's mom announces.

I smile shyly and thank her. I hope she's right! I know I said I didn't care if I medaled and just wanted to skate well, but with how incredibly I just skated, well… I guess I just want my best to be good enough. A medal would prove that it is!

# CHAPTER 28

## *The Waiting Game*

Watching the rest of my group only makes me more nervous. I thought my nerves would go away after I was done, but apparently this works just like testing; the nerves probably won't go away until I get my results. I pick out two skaters who I thought were incredible and much better skaters than I am. I didn't see the two skaters before me, so it's hard to say if they were better. Using those skaters, my math tells me I should place somewhere between third and fifth. Not bad for my first competition! Maybe even a bronze medal! I try hard to not let myself get too excited; I don't want to disappoint myself.

"Khalli, would you like to go look at the booths again? We can come back to see Yana skate," Mom asks.

"Absolutely!" I jump up.

"Okay, but she can't go yet," Dad interjects.

"Why not?"

"Because I haven't given you any spending money."

"But I'll be with Mom—"

"Yeah, but you'll need this," Dad cuts me off and hands me the beautiful coin purse that I picked out earlier.

I jump up to hug him. I knew my dad couldn't say no!

"Your mom and I are so proud of you, Khalli, not just for how well you skated, but for how hard you have been working. We are so impressed with your determination to bounce back after the ice show! Regardless of if you medal or not, we want you to have something from your first competition."

I give each of my parents a massive hug. They're amazing!

"And there's twenty dollars in there," Dad whispers with a wink.

Oh my God—they are *really* amazing!

"Just in case you want that T-shirt I saw you eyeing up before," he hints.

I never even said anything about the competition shirt! How did he know?

"Oh, I really do want it, I just didn't want to ask!" I exclaim.

Mom and I browse through the booths, admiring all the incredible skating merchandise. I really want a competition T-shirt to wear to school, but first I want to make sure there isn't anything else I want more.

"Khalli! Khalli!" Yana comes running up behind me with her skates on, looking fully ready to take the ice. Coach Marie is in tow, her face devoid of any emotion.

"Your results are up!" Yana nearly shouts ecstatically.

"How'd I do?" I look back and forth between Yana and Coach Marie.

My coach's face is still blank, and Yana's smile doesn't give anything away other than that she's excited I get to finally see my results.

"You'll have to check for yourself. Come follow us," my coach says with a calm smile.

I practically run over to the postings. My results are taped on the wall directly over my skating order sheet, so I know exactly where to go. There's a big crowd of skaters huddled around tightly. I rock up to my tiptoes to try to see better, squinting in full force—but no luck. I guess I'll have to wait my turn.

Skaters in front of me are screaming, laughing, and crying—both tears of joy and frustration. The emotion radiating from my group is electric. I watch both in awe and impatience, waiting anxiously for my turn to see the sheet.

The thirty seconds of waiting feels like an eternity before I finally make my way to the front of the pack. Coach Marie is directly behind me, Yana and my mom are waiting along the side of the group.

I start from the bottom, slowly moving my eyes from last place upwards. Where's my name? The higher my eyes go up the list, the more excited I become. And then…"*2. Khalli Davies, Berger Lake.*"

Second place? Oh my God!

"I got *second*?" I practically shout at Coach Marie.

"You did!" Coach Marie pulls me into a massive hug. "I'm so proud of you, Khalli!"

She gives me a moment to take everything in before continuing. Then she steps back, looking me square in the eyes. "I want you to look at these scores closer."

The buzz of excitement has faded, so we step up to the results sheet together. She explains how each judge gives me a ranking based on how I skated.

"And if you look here, this score shows that you actually initially tied for first place!"

"What?"

"You were beautiful out there, Khalli! And you really kept your head in the game. Your final placement came when the scores were added," she points at the rankings of three judges, "and the Total of Majority score was determined. You only took second by essentially one point! You should be beyond proud for your first competition!"

I can't stop beaming! Yana and my mom give me huge hugs, and Coach Marie quickly explains to my mom where I'll go to get my medal and photos.

Then turning to me, she says, "It's almost time for Yana to skate, so we need to go. But I'm so proud of you! You've earned this!"

I give Yana a hurried hug and wish her luck and then skip to the bleachers to get my dad for my medal ceremony!

# CHAPTER 29

## *Not All That Glitters Is Gold, Silver Sparkles Just as Much*

I can't stop beaming as I stand on the podium. The skater in third place bows her head to receive her medal—I had totally pegged her as one of the skaters who was better than me. This is something I have zero problem being wrong about!

"In second place, Khalli Davies!"

Everyone claps and cheers for me as I bow my head to receive my stunning silver medal!

"Congratulations, Khalli!" The announcer shakes my hand.

I cannot stop beaming. I have no words to reply to her. I just smile boldly in response.

I turn to watch the first place skater accept her gold medal and instantly notice her wet tights. This is the girl who fell during warm-up, the one I had written off as someone I could beat. I guess a bad warm-up really doesn't mean a bad performance. Tucking that into the back of my mind as a future reminder to myself if I ever have a poor warm-up, I turn to congratulate my competitors, making a mental note of their names and faces. I'm sure I'll compete against them again and want to know whom I'm up against if I see their names in my group. Next time I want to beat Nellie Blancherd, the first place skater with the wet tights.

"Let me see this!" Dad enthusiastically lifts my medal to inspect it. "Khalli, this is beautiful! Look at the detail! And the shine!"

Mom swoons over my medal just as much. I think it's safe to say my parents are proud.

I smile boldly. I cannot believe I took second place in my very first competition!

"Khalli, Yana just started her warm up. Why don't you change, we'll put your bags in the car, and then we'll come back to watch Yana. She's at the end of her group, so you have enough time," Mom suggests.

I agree and skip off happily to gather my things and change. When I come back, Mom and Dad are holding out a competition T-shirt for me, complete with my name printed across the back!

"Why don't you put this on, along with your medal, of course, and then we'll drop your stuff in the car. I've just checked, there are five more skaters before Yana. You have time."

I squeal a big thank-you to my parents as I run back to change my shirt.

At the car, I open the back door to toss my bags on the seat next to where I'll sit.

"Let's put them in the trunk, Khalli."

Dad pops open the trunk. I head to the back of our sedan and lift my bags only to set them down on two duffel bags.

"What's this?"

Mom and Dad glance at each other with sneaky smiles, and it becomes clear they've been keeping a secret.

"We've booked a hotel for tonight, one with an indoor water park. Your swimsuit is packed—and you are fully ready for a one-night spring break getaway! We're so proud of how hard you've been working, Khalli. You dedicated your entire spring break to the ice and made so much progress in just a week. Coach Marie said you pushed yourself to the limits in your lessons and consistently surprised her with your drive. So tonight your mom and I want to teach you a lesson. It's the 'work hard, play hard' lesson. You've more than earned a little getaway. Time to learn how to play hard!" Dad laughs.

I don't even know what to say!

"You almost busted me booking this the other day! The day you couldn't stop smacking your peanut butter!" Mom pokes at me, tickling me until I nearly fall over laughing.

I have the greatest parents in the world. I really thought we weren't going to do anything for spring break—but instead I got to spend every day at the rink, compete, and win silver, and now a getaway!

I wrap my arms around them as we head into the rink to cheer on my friend. I snuggle up with Mom in the bleachers just in time to hear the announcer.

"Representing Berger Lake, please welcome… Ahryana Andrews!"

I scream for Yana at the top of my lungs! I cannot wait to watch my friend shine.

Special thanks to Surya Bonaly! It is an honor and a privilege getting to share a bit of your journey with my readers. Your story is such an inspiration, and your accomplishments are unparalleled. Thank you for allowing me to share insight into your road to success!

Readers, you can learn even more about the incredible achievements of Surya Bonaly! Look for her children's book "Fearless Heart" in stores in early 2022!

Coming soon!

*Taking the Ice*
*Ice Cold Summer*

# ABOUT THE AUTHOR

At the age of ten, Allye Ritt began a figure skating hobby that would eventually turn into a lifelong career. Allye is now a seven-time US Figure Skating Gold Medalist, an International Dance Medalist, and has also achieved the Skate Canada Gold Dance test. She has skated professionally around the world on three different continents and currently coaches full-time as a career. She is a rated coach through the Professional Skaters Association and also serves as the director for an area figure skating program. Allye thoroughly enjoys guiding her students as they grow in the sport of figure skating and loves watching their confidence blossom as they excel.

In her free time, you will find her in an ice rink, reading, at the gym, or spending time with her husband, Jeffrey, as well as their two cats, Bakyn and Tatyr. As a former middle and high school teacher for German and history, Allye holds a deep passion for learning, especially about historical and modern cultures. This passion has led to a genuine desire to see as much of the world as possible. Together, Allye and Jeffrey love travelling and taking in new places and experiences whenever they have the opportunity.

Milton Keynes UK
Ingram Content Group UK Ltd.
UKHW041421030923
427969UK00001B/91

9 781638 850700